HIGH PRAISE FOR 2008 SPUR AWARD WINNER JOHNNY D. BOGGS!

"One of the best Western writers at work today!"
—*Publishers Weekly*

"Boggs...writes with a finely honed sense of character and a keen eye for detail..."
—*Booklist*

"Boggs is unparalleled at evoking the gritty reality of the Old West."
—*The Shootist*

"A terrific writer."
—*Roundup*

"Johnny D. Boggs has a keen ability to interlace historically accurate information amid a cast of descriptive characters and circumstances."
—*Cowboy Chronicle*

"Boggs, one of the most dependable Western writers working today, delivers again with this charming and exciting over-the-hill adventure."
—*Booklist*

Doubtful Cañon

Johnny D.
Boggs

LEISURE BOOKS NEW YORK CITY

A LEISURE BOOK®

July 2009

Published by special arrangement with Golden West Literary Agency.

Dorchester Publishing Co., Inc.
200 Madison Avenue
New York, NY 10016

ISBN 10: 0-8439-6275-5
ISBN 13: 978-0-8439-6275-8
E-ISBN: 978-1-4285-0705-0

The name "Leisure Books" and the stylized "L" with design are trademarks of Dorchester Publishing Co., Inc.

Printed in the United States of America.

10 9 8 7 6 5 4 3 2 1

Visit us on the web at www.dorchesterpub.com.

*For the teachers, staff, and students
At Children's Garden Montessori*

Doubtful Cañon

Chapter One

This is the story the albino man told.

You kids ain't never heard the like, never seen such sights, but I'll swear on ever' Bible in Shakespeare that what you're 'bout to hear is pure gospel. Burned in my memory it is, engraved like the etchin's on this here pistol of mine. Ain't no way I can forget a minute of it, and I've tried. Tried long and hard for . . . what, two decades or so. Some of it, I mean. Parts of it, though, I just gots to remember. Gots to. Remember ever' last detail.

Ain't no tale for the squeamish, so if you ain't up to it, light a shuck for home now. Once I get started, I ain't stoppin', but, if you stay, and if you believe what I'm fixin' to tell you, and if you wanna share a fortune in gold by helpin' help me find it, well, I'm in the market for some pardners and y'all look to fill the bill. Even you, li'l' girlie.

Now the time I tell 'bout be a whole lot diff'rent than the one you be used to. Territory hereabouts is civilized, more or less, after twenty years. Wasn't no railroad. A body'd be hard pressed to find even a rail in Texas, I reckon, and nothin' down here in New Mexico Territory. Even this here town wasn't nothin' but cactus and rocks. Wasn't nothin'. Nothin' but rattle-snakes.

And Apaches.

Apaches had been at peace with us. Not that you can trust no Apache, and 'em truces had always been about as shaky as a scairt petticoat's hands, but things might have gone different if it hadn't been for the Army. Well, not the whole Army. Just that one fool lieutenant. And those red devils that had taken John Ward's cattle and kidnapped his little boy.

So the Army goes and sends this snot-nosed kid with about as much experience as you three shirt tails. George Bascom. I'd met the blue belly oncet. Didn't think much of him. But the Army sent him and sixty troopers to Apache Pass just across the mountains in Arizona Territory, it bein' New Mexico Territory back then. So Mr. Bascom arranges a little parley with Cochise. You recollect that name? Might be a little afore your time. No? Yeah. I figured y'all may have heard of him. Big chief among the Apaches, he was. Big medicine. Bigger medicine than any Apache then or since. Mangas Coloradas. Victorio. Nana. All of 'em combined couldn't match Cochise for bravery, cunnin', and savagery. Friendly at the time, Cochise was, but some of those fool high-graders down Tucson way had tol' the fool lieutenant that Cochise was to blame for it all. Cochise, or his Apaches, had raided Mr. Ward's ranch, stolen off his son, they said. Pack of lies that was. Lies that would get a bunch of men, women, and young 'uns . . . white and Mex . . . kilt. Maybe some of your kinfolk.

Anyway, Bascom had invited Cochise and six of his men to come talk. Under a flag of truce, I tell you, but oncet the bootlicker had those Apaches in his tent, he tried to arrest 'em. Said they'd hang for what they had done if they didn't turn over that boy and the cattle. Well, Cochise ain't no fool, and he didn't take no threats from nobody. He whips out his knife, slits a hole in the canvas, makes good his escape. But the soldier boys capture the other Apaches.

You gots to understand that the Apaches don't think like us white folks. Or maybe they do. Maybe they's just as bad as the worst of our breed. Cochise, he wants his pals back, and the only way he knows how to do it is to capture some *gringos*. Have an exchange. You give me my men and I'll give you these three white folks. That kind of thing, iffen you gets my meanin'. Bascom, fool that he was, he said nothin' doin', and that riled Cochise somethin' fierce.

That commenced all the bloodshed. Apaches started liftin' hair. Bascom up and hanged his six prisoners, some of 'em bein' kinfolk to Cochise, which he had no call to do. And that was it. Cochise took to war, and, when an Apache declares war, 'tain't no fleetin' thing. It's a straight-out fight. Savagerous. It's mean and ugly and hot and long. *Long.* Almost a dozen years passed by, a dozen bloody years, afore the Army ever made peace with Cochise. How old are you, li'l' girlie? Yeah, you'd been still in your diapers by the time old Cochise give up the fight. You two boys, your ol' papas might have been no older than you are now when it all started. But I was a man full growed back then. Caught right dag smack in the middle. Lucky to have my hair, I am.

The fracas at Apache Pass had happened back in February, a few months after Mr. Ward lost his longhorns and kid. That had been in Eighteen and Sixty-One, and I warrant y'all knows what happened in that year back East. In April, just a couple months after Cochise went on the prod, 'em good ol' boys in South Caroliny opened fire on Fort Sumter. The big war was on. War of the Rebellion. Civil War . . . criminy, like there was anything *civil* about that! War for Southern Independence. War Between the States. Whatever you wanna call it. I was about to be out of a job.

Ever heard of John Butterfield? Didn't expect so. Y'all think the Southern Pacific's been around here forever, but it ain't. I done tol' y'all that much. No, in the year of 'Sixty-One, if a body wanted to post a letter to Californy, he had to send it all the way around the Cape or put it aboard one of Mr. John Butterfield's Concord stagecoaches. I worked for Mr. Butterfield. Never been 'board a ship in all my life, never even seen no ocean, and most of the water I seen wouldn't fill a canteen. Might have been the best years of my life, workin' for that glorious enterprise for 'em three, four years.

All the way from Missouri through Arkansas and the Indian Territory, Texas, New Mexico Territory, and on to Californy. The Overland Mail Company, run by Mr. Butterfield. Twice-a-week mail service gettin' your letters and passengers all the way to Californy in twenty-five days or less. I think they said it come to somethin' like two thousand eight hundred miles. Reckon I was responsible for 'bout one hundred twenty of 'em, from Eagle Springs to Franklin, which is the name El Paso went by in those olden times I'm tellin' y'all 'bout.

No, I wasn't no jehu. I didn't drive them temperamental mules. No, I was the guard. Messenger or conductor, we called it. Had me a muzzle-loadin' shotgun for any bandits that might show his ugly head. And a Walker Colt, which I lost in a poker game at Dead Man's Hole. Wisht I still had that old hoss pistol for it kicked like a cannon and could drop even a buffalo. Later, I got me an Enfield rifle, and the April I'm tellin' y'all 'bout, the April that saw the war begin between the Yankees and the Rebels, the April I knowed I was 'bout to be hung out to dry without no job, by then I had me a brace of Navy Colts, which Mr. John James Giddings gots me outfitted with.

Texas Division. Mr. Giddings ran that ship. Texas Division of the Overland Mail, but with the South leavin' the Union, and Texas joinin' up with the Confederacy, John Butterfield had no choice but to shut down the Overland, so Mr. Giddings up and sold off all he could. Come out with thirty thousand dollars in gold coin, a right smart of money, then and now. His bosses told him to make sure the Confederates didn't seize that chunk of change, and ordered him to take that money all the way to Californy. Union territory.

Giddings was a brave man, Union blue to the core, said he'd get the job done. He hired Sam Golden as his driver and me to guard. So we went ridin' on what might have been the last official journey for Butterfield's stagecoach line. When we hit Mesilla, we learnt word that Cochise's Apaches was raidin' all over that part of the country, so Giddings hired us two other gunmen. A Mexican named Enrique Valdez and a Wisconsin man called Bruce. Don't know if that was his first name or his last name, or just some name he chose for hisself, but he was a good hand with a gun. So was the Mex. We figured they'd get tested, certain sure.

Loaded up with powder and lead, water . . . not

much for victuals other than hardtack, jerky, some coffee, which we figured we'd never get a chance to make . . . we rode off west from Mesilla into this desert country. Didn't see no sign of Apaches, hardly no sign of white folks, as we raised dust to Cooke's Spring. Then Soldier's Farewell. Peaceable things was. Peaceable and quiet. Reckon I started to relax a mite, but then we come to Stein's Peak.

Well, I didn't relax no more. Come to think on it, I ain't had me one peaceful moment since.

We was supposed to get a fresh team. Used to feed the passengers on the regular runs at that station, but there wasn't no passengers, just us guards, the jehu and Mr. Giddings. Wasn't no stockmen or stationkeeper at Stein's Peak, either. Not alive. No stock. No grub. Nothin'. Not even the station. Not much, I mean. Charred timbers and blacked rocks, the walls fallin' down. Ashes. Blood and dead folks. Ugly.

I smelt the smoke afore I seen it snakin' its way into the blue sky, so I called down to the boys inside the coach to be ready, but you just can't be ready for what we come 'cross. Ever smelt a human body afire, kids? Smells just like a burnt steak, it does, only it don't make you hungry. Might even make a man swear off eatin' meat of any kind. Turn a stomach, it does, by the stench alone. And have mercy if you see what the body looks like . . . what an Apache'll do. Even made our jehu scatter his breakfast all over the driver's box, and Sam Golden had been in the territory for some ten, fifteen years. Apaches ain't got no mercy in their souls, and there ain't nobody nowhere in this world that knows how to torture better than one of 'em savages. And amongst the Apaches, the Cherry Cows, which is what we called the Chiricahuas, they was the brutalest.

Stein's Peak station had always been fortified. Rock walls. Plenty of good men with guns. Had to be, this deep in Apache country, this far from civilized folks, and I always figured that 'em Indians would have raided somethin' that looked a mite easier. Cooke's Spring. Maybe Dragoon Springs. But Cochise and his boys was always full of surprises.

They sure had surprised the folks at Stein's Peak station.

We pulled the Concord to a stop in the middle of the station's grounds, and I climbed down from my perch while Sam Golden blowed chunks of salt pork and beans out of his gizzard.

"My word . . . ," Mr. Giddings began as he stepped out of the stage, then leaned back, knees bucklin', and fumbled in his pockets for some handkerchief. Bloodier'n a gander-pullin', what we was seein'. Mr. Giddings wiped his face, which kept gettin' paler, whiter'n even me, knockin' off that bell crown hat he wore. "My word," he said again, only this time much softer.

"Ain't no *word* for it," I tells him, pullin' my bandanna up over my nose and mouth, and went to take a look-see, keepin' my Enfield rifle ready, cocked, my finger on that trigger.

Bruce and the Mex took care of the poor, dumb soul that had had the misfortune to get hisself captured still alive. Red vermin had hung 'im by his ankles over a bed of hot coals. Well, no point in tellin' you young 'uns about that. They also pulled out the burnin' body of the stationkeeper. Least, we figgered him to be the keeper. Couldn't rightly be sure, black as the body was burnt.

I found two other bodies, filled with arrows. Looked like bloated porcupines, they did. Ghastly.

That's what Sam Golden called it, oncet he got his voice back. Reckon that's about the sum of it.

The Mex and Bruce, they spread out to scout things a mite, 'emselves, and Mr. Giddings, he recovered and put his hat back on, walked over toward me. Like I said, Giddings, he wasn't no coward. It's just that sights like that'll shock even the most hardened rapscallion that ever breathed good air.

"Is there anything we can do for them, Mister Grey?" Giddings asked me.

Shakin' my head, I pulled down my bandanna and spat. Bitter taste it left in my mouth. Like gall. "Bury 'em if you want to risk your own life, and that gold," is what I tol' him. I pointed the Enfield's barrel at the two gents felled by dozens of Cherry Cow arrows. "This couldn't have happened too long ago. Turkey vultures and coyot's ain't got to the bodies yet."

"Well, we cannot leave them," Mr. Giddings said. "Not like this."

"Sure we can," I tells him. "Lessen, like I said, you wanna join 'em."

"Poisoned the well!" the Mex cried out, and he let a string of curses fly out of his mouth, speakin' Mex and English.

I cussed my ownself. Our mules was plumb tuckered out, and I didn't see how they could get us through the Peloncillo Mountains. Not without fresh water. We needed a fresh team, but the Apaches had taken care of that.

"Smart thing, Mister Giddings," I said, "might be to turn back."

"I have my orders," he said. "Besides, surely the Army's in the field."

My notions ran contrary to his'ns. "Nearest fort's Buchanan. Maybe Aravaipa . . . no, they're callin' it

Breckinridge these days . . . but 'em two posts be a long way from this here pike, sir. And all 'em soldier boys gots their hands full. Closest town's Tucson, but that might as well be Washin'ton City, 'cause 'em miles'll be the hardest you ever traveled."

"We're not turning back," he said. Man had gumption, a belly full of it. "Perhaps the next station will have fresh livestock."

"Doubtful," I tol' him, and once again I used my Enfield for a pointer, this time aimin' it toward the Peloncillos. "You know how come they named that Doubtful Cañon?"

He knowed. Had to know, him bein' a big man with the Overland, but he didn't answer. So I tells him. "Doubtful," I said, "anybody'll get through that alive if the Apaches is ornery." I let out a little laugh, though there wasn't nary a thing funny, and waved my hand at all the death and blood and smoke and ruin amongst us. "In case you ain't noticed, sir, the Apaches is ornery. Ornery and then some."

"We proceed," he said, louder this time, and I noticed that the Mex, Bruce, and old Sam had gathered about us. Sam Golden rubbed the rest of the vomit off his face, and the Mex crossed hisself. Bruce didn't blink, didn't nod, just stood there. He'd dealt hisself into the game and wasn't foldin'. Couldn't fold. He was a hired gunman. Reckon you'd call me that, too.

"We got some water," Sam Golden said. "I'll let the mules drink a mite. They've cooled down enough by now."

"Good man," Giddings said. "While you tend the team, the rest of us will bury these poor victims of unholy barbarity."

"Bury 'em?" I belted out. "You off your nut, sir?" I

jabbed the Enfield barrel toward the slob those fiends had tortured. "You want your brains to boil? Wanna beg to die? 'Cause that's what'll happen if 'em butchers come back!"

"Why should they come back, Mister Grey?" Mr. Giddings had removed his coat and waistcoat, foldin' 'em up neatly. "They have no knowledge of our presence. We have fired no shots, given no cries of alarm. The horses and mules are gone, and there is nothing left here but . . . but. . . ." He couldn't control the shudder, but it didn't stop him. "It is my Christian duty to see these men are given a proper burial, or as proper as we can under the trying circumstances. It is your Christian duty, too."

The Mex, he said the only thing. "Sí." And crossed hisself once more.

Ask me, it was a mistake, but I wasn't nothin' more'n a hired hand, so Mr. Giddings barked out the orders, even if barkin' wasn't his nature, and we did his biddin's. With only one shovel and two picks, one of 'em burned and blackened, that the Cherry Cows had left amongst all that ruin, between us, and not all of us as full of Christian charity and decency as Mr. John James Giddings, we made fast work of that burial. Only dug one grave, and it pretty shallow, and we had nothin' to spare as shrouds, no wood around that wasn't burnt or part of the stagecoach for a coffin, or Cherry Cow arrows, so we just dragged the dead to the pit and covered 'em with sand. Doubt if it would keep the wolves offen 'em, but I didn't tell the boss man that. Mr. Giddings made a little cross out of rocks to mark the grave, and he kept his prayer short. He spouted out some Scripture. Said it was from Psalms, but I'd have to take his word for it. Maybe he was prayin' for us, I thought, as much as them guys the Apaches had kilt, 'cause when he said . . . "Yea, though I walk through the valley of the shadow of death, I will fear no evil." . . . I figured that's exactly where we was headed. The Valley of the Shadow of Death. Only we wasn't walkin', but ridin' in a stagecoach. Ridin' right through Doubtful Cañon and a passel of Chiricahua Apaches on the warpath. But *fear no evil?* You show me a white man who says he ain't afeared of Apaches, and I'll show you a liar or a fool.

Mr. Giddings tossed some dust on that pit, and we was done with it. We all made a beeline for the Concord. The Mex asked if he could ride atop the coach with Sam, 'stead of me. Reckon he needed some air. Couldn't blame him none. I let him.

That's how come I'm still here to tell you young 'uns this here story. Sam Golden and the Mex rode atop. Me and Bruce and Mr. Giddings sat in the coach, and we lit out for Doubtful Cañon just up the road.

Doubtful Cañon.

And death.

Chapter Two

When the albino man who called himself Whitey Grey paused to wash down a mouthful of beans with tepid water from a gourd canteen, my best friend peppered him with questions.

"What happened next? Did the Apaches attack you? How'd you get out of the fight? Where's that gold? What happened, Mister Grey? You got to let us know what happened next!"

Whitey Grey had set the hook deep in Ian Spencer Henry! Well, I guess he had pretty much hooked Jasmine and me, too.

"What happened?" Jasmine Allison asked, a little more polite, a lot less enthusiastic than Ian Spencer Henry, while I tried to formulate my own questions, organize my own thoughts. Pa had taught me to be inquisitive, but patient, and never to act recklessly or ask ill-thought-out questions, but my father didn't hold much influence over me on that October day. He hadn't for a while.

"I have an airtight of peaches," I said. "They're good. Really good, and sweet, full of juice."

"Sure, sure, sure, that's mighty fine, mighty fine. You're a top hand . . . what's that you say your name is? Jack? Jack. Yeah, I've knowed me a handful of Jacks, includin' Black Jack McKeithan and One-Eared Jack O'Donnell, but you're toppin' ever' last one of 'em. Peaches! Ain't that somethin'. Sure can't finish my story on no empty stomach. Here, let me open that there airtight with this here knife of mine. And don't fret none, young 'uns, 'cause once I et these here peaches, I'll let you know how come I'm alive, how come that gold's still buried yonder in Doubtful Cañon, how come I'm willin' to take on three children as pardners. Won't leave out no blood and thunder, but it ain't no stretcher, I'm tellin' y'all. It's the gospel. Didn't get it out of no half-dime novel. Boys, li'l' girlie . . . I lived it. Almost died it."

Whitey Grey had chiseled himself into our lives that morning when Ian Spencer Henry, Jasmine Allison, and I made our surreptitious journey to the Lady Macbeth Mine for school. It wasn't a real school. Shakespeare had no school. Not really. The town had no church either, a fact that had caused me pause after hearing Whitey Grey's comment about swearing on every Bible in town. I doubt if there were six Good Books in the whole town, including the one in the old Lady Macbeth shack from which some miner had torn out pages to patch holes in the adobe walls.

We lived in a raw, hot, brutal mining town in New Mexico, a few miles south of Lordsburg and the Southern Pacific rails. My father had come to Shakespeare to start a newspaper—the Shakespeare *Globe*, he'd told Mama he'd call it, wondering if any silver miner would get the joke. For a year he had worked at the Shakespeare Gold and Silver Mining and Milling Company, saving his money until he had enough to become Shakespeare's first journalist. Only before he got the first edition published, my mother and baby sisters took sick. Diphtheria, Mr. Shankin said. Mr. Shankin was no doctor—Shakespeare lacked one of those, as well—but he came as close to anyone in town, and whatever the disease, whatever his diagnosis, my mother and siblings had been called to Glory within a week. Therefore, the Potter press collected dust, and my father spent his time brooding, not speaking, not even to me until he discovered the power of John Barleycorn.

We picture mining towns of the West as lawless establishments, regular Sodoms, and Shakespeare certainly lived up to such description. On my eleventh birthday, I had watched Curly Bill Brocious gun down some cardsharp on Avon Street over a three dollar bet, then spit out the most foul curses imaginable as he paid two Mexican laborers five dollars each to bury the cheat. Such was the law in Shakespeare. We had no constable, no marshal, and rarely if ever saw a sheriff's deputy, but if you killed a man, you had to bury him. That was our Golden Rule. With the desert heat, it certainly made murder less attractive, Pa used to say, before he took to drink.

Yet while silver miners and boomtown parasites might not have much need of religion, they often display a charitable side, so the entrepreneurs behind the National Mail and Transportation Company, the Stratford Hotel, and Shankin General Merchandise led the charge to form a subscription school and hire the would-be editor, Russell Dunivan, as schoolmaster. "It'll take Russell's mind off his tragic loss," Mr. Shankin said, "give him a new purpose." My father happily accepted, and thirteen children from ages eight to fifteen filled our home on the outskirts of town.

Of course, the good citizens of Shakespeare didn't know the extent of my father's depression, or his need for liquor. The subscription fees paid for his whiskey. At first, he'd pass out *McGuffey's Readers* to students, the extent of his lessons. Then he'd drink. Later, he just drank himself into a stupor without bothering to effect some semblance of teaching the three R's. So I'd try to fill that void. Was it family pride? Shame? A desire to educate? Honestly I don't know. The older boys laughed at me and walked out, but some of the younger ones stayed . . . for a while. Within a year, most students had stopped coming, and the Southern Pacific had put the National Mail and Transportation Company out of business. There was no more subscription school— really, there never had been one—so Pa found his drinkin' money (when he didn't just steal the scamper juice) elsewhere, but I kept trying to be the great educator.

That's because of Jasmine Allison.

Back when there had been at least a façade of a school, Jasmine's mother had no money for the subscription, and even those charitable people trying to help out my father had limits. Jasmine's mother worked in one of the cribs, and her father (or so the story went) had been Cornwall Dan. In November of 1880, Cornwall Dan and a San Simon cowboy named Harley King had been hanged in the Grant House's dining room. King's crime was horse theft, Cornwall Dan was executed for being a pest, and everyone in Shakespeare knew the timbers in the

Grant House's roof to be among the strongest in the county, a suitable substitute for the gallows.

Offspring of a hanged border ruffian and a soiled dove, Jasmine Allison was ostracized by everyone, it seems, but Ian Spencer Henry and me.

Even had her mother been able to afford it, Jasmine wasn't allowed to attend school, and I took exception to that. She was a pretty girl, dark-haired, dark-eyed, strong-willed. I found her beautiful, and—unlike most of the children of miners, legitimate business-men, and parasites—she wanted to learn. So I be-came her tutor, with Ian Spencer Henry serving as my assistant.

Every day, we'd meet at the Lady Macbeth Mine, long played out and deserted except for tarantu-las, scorpions, and rattlesnakes. After too many cave-ins and not enough pay dirt, the owners had closed it up even before Shakespeare came into ex-istence. Some—even Mr. Shankin—labeled the mine haunted, and located on the far southern tip of town, few grown-ups ever ventured that way. Perfect place, I thought, for a secret school.

That afternoon, Allison, Ian Spencer Henry, and I were walking toward the abandoned mine when we met Whitey Grey for the first time.

"What are you kids doin' here? Get out! Get away or I'll rip out your hearts and et 'em!"

He barged out of the Lady Macbeth's entrance, and, for a second, the three of us froze. He wore duck trousers stuffed inside scuffed boots of two differ-ent colors and sizes, soiled braces, and a dust-covered, green-and-white plaid shirt missing several buttons and its bib front, a faded calico bandanna, hat bat-tered beyond recognition, and an ivory-handled Colt stuck in his waistband. Even at the distance of several rods, I could tell his face was savagely pock-marked, and his hair and thick mustache were un-kempt. I couldn't call him a big man. Later I would realize he was rather small, and he dressed—with the exception of the fancy revolver—and looked like most miners in town.

Except he was an albino.

The stark white hair ... the skin just as pale ... eyes almost dead, inhuman. When he came charging out of that mine, screaming that he'd eat our hearts, even though educated in reason and enlight-enment, I couldn't help but fear that Mr. Shankin and everyone else in Shakespeare had been right. The Lady Macbeth was haunted, and here, as proof, charged a ghost. So we did what any twelve-year-olds would do.

We skedaddled.

Dropping in the dust the sack containing a pail of leftover beans and airtight of peaches that I had pro-cured for Jasmine, I whirled, grabbed her hand, and led a not-so-gallant retreat. Out of the corner of my eye, I spotted Ian Spencer Henry dive beside the rock wall and disappear through a coyote hole. That's when I tripped, sending Jasmine and myself sprawl-ing into the dust. Hearing the white man's curses, and his footfalls, I screamed Jasmine's name and crawled underneath an overturned ore cart, barely propped up on a boulder, the opening about as small as the coyote hole through which Ian Spencer Henry had made his escape. Jasmine followed, and we waited, staring, hearts pounding, trying to catch our breath. Dust and dirt caused my eyes to tear, and I realized I had picked a terrible hiding spot.

A moment later, I found myself staring at an un-matched pair of boots, one the color of dried blood, missing the inside mule-ear pull, the other dusty black, one with a squared toe, the other with no toe at all, just a frayed, filthy sock sticking out.

"Hey, there, you young 'uns. Don't run. Ain't no need to hide. I ain't gonna hurt y'all none. Just gave me a fright is all. Come back here. Come out from under there afore that ol' thing falls down on you. Iffen that happens, you be dead certain sure. Suffocate you, it will, 'cause I ain't strong enough to lift it offen you. I ain't no outlaw, no monster. Here. I picked up your . . . what is that? Beans? Criminy, beans and a tin of somethin'.'" He smacked his lips. Then, with a heavy grunt, knee joints popping, he flattened himself on the ground and stared into our frightened faces.

"I'm your friend, kids. Name's Grey. Whitey Grey. Come on out. Let's talk a mite."

We did what any twelve-year-olds would do when ordered by a grown-up. We obeyed.

Whitey Grey dusted off our clothes as best as he could, although his efforts left us dirtier, and reluctantly handed Jasmine the sack of beans and peaches. "Where's that other boy?" Whitey Grey demanded. "He ain't run off, has he? Why, the way he scrambled through that li'l' hole! Can you fetch your friend back, young 'uns? I got a proposition to make y'all!"

"Ian!" I yelled. "Ian Spencer Henry! Come back here."

Nothing.

"Come on, Ian Spencer Henry!" Jasmine echoed.

"Hey, there!" Squatting, Whitey Grey peered closely at Jasmine, his monstrous eyes squinting. "Criminy, you ain't no boy. You're a gal."

"Ian Spencer Henry!" Jasmine called again, ignoring the white-skinned man's observation. "Are you yellow?"

"He's not going to hurt us!" I yelled, though I couldn't say that I had completely made up my mind yet.

At last, there came a faint reply. "I ain't getting my heart ripped out and ate up!"

"I was just funnin', boy!" the strange man called out, and let out a little chuckle. "Funnin' is all. I need . . . I need . . . need me some pardners." The laughter died abruptly, and the pale face hardened with seriousness. "For thirty thousand dollars in . . ."—he lowered his voice—"gold."

"Gold?" I asked, a little too loud for Whitey Grey's liking, because he cringed, his face now angry, and gave me a chilling look with his dead eyes before he looked around to make sure no one had heard. There was no one around but us.

A fortune in gold, I thought. Shakespeare was a silver town. Most attempts at finding enough gold to make mining worthwhile had failed, but the word had prompted Ian Spencer Henry to pop his head through the small opening in the fence. Seeing that Jasmine and I were still alive, our hearts remaining inside our chests, he snaked his way through, brushed off the dirt from his trousers and shirt, and approached us tentatively.

"Let's get out of the sun." Whitey Grey led us to the opening of the Lady Macbeth. Once inside, he sat cross-legged facing the entrance, and we gathered around him.

"You gonna eat 'em there beans?" he asked.

When Jasmine shrugged, and I understood his

meaning, I took the sack from Jasmine's hands and passed the grub to him. He withdrew the pail from the sack, returned the airtight of peaches to me, and attacked the cold beans with a vengeance.

"What about the gold?" Ian Spencer Henry asked.

Since my family's arrival in Shakespeare, Ian Spencer Henry had been my best friend. He turned out to be an outcast, much like Jasmine, much like, after the Dunivan tragedy, me. His father worked in the assay office in town while his mother lived somewhere in Michigan with his stepfather—at twelve, I didn't quite understand the scandal of this—and to hear Ian Spencer Henry talk, his father didn't know he even existed, keeping his nose buried in books and ore. My best friend passed his time reading the five-penny dreadfuls Mr. Shankin peddled, and, when he had memorized the text of those stories, he would sell them to eager miners for a profit of two cents, things costing higher, even half-dime novels, in a rawhide mining town like Shakespeare, New Mexico.

He stood about my size, with sandier hair and green eyes instead of my blue, prone to go off on a whim or a dare while I remained the cautious one. As voraciously as he read, his true calling came in math. He could cipher figures better than his father, or anyone else, at the assay office. I figured he'd grow up to be about as wealthy as Colonel William G. Boyle, whose mines had brought Shakespeare to new life back in 'Seventy-Nine. Although good at mathematics, Ian Spencer Henry had little interest in figures. At age twelve, like most boys his age, he longed for adventure.

"The gold?" Ian Spencer Henry—I never called him anything but his full name, and never heard anyone call him different—repeated when he got no answer.

This time, Whitey Grey lifted his rump off his rock seat, and let out a loud fart. Jasmine rolled her eyes. Ian Spencer Henry grabbed his nose and gagged. I don't remember what I did. Patiently we waited for the smell to fade, for the white-skinned man to finish his tale.

"I know where there's a fortune in gold," the albino man finally said. "Only I need help in gettin' it. Pardners. You young 'uns be game?"

"You bet!" Ian Spencer Henry blurted out, unaware that I was tugging on his shirt sleeve, begging him to slow down, to think this thing through. For all I knew, this odd man really did intend on cutting out our hearts and eating them, burying our bodies deep in an abandoned mine where no one would ever dream or dare to look.

"What's the split?" It was Jasmine who broke the silence, who suddenly commanded the albino man's attention. He laughed, and I choked down my fear.

"You gots sass. I likes that. It's thirty thousand dollars. Gold coin. It bein' my gold, and what with me havin' better'n twenty years invested in the deal, I figger on me gettin' twenty-five of it, but that's five thousand dollars to split amongst your own-selves. Five thousand dollars. But afore I go tellin' you my story, you got to answer me a few questions. Such as . . . how come you kids ain't in school?"

"We're orphans!"

The voice surprised me—for it was my own. I saw my share of five thousand dollars as a ticket out of the purgatory in which I had found myself trapped. I could put Shakespeare and my drunkard father far behind me. Finally I could bury him, alongside Ma, Patsy, and Kaye, at least in my memory, my reasoning.

"Orphans! Jack, we ain't. . . ."

I kicked Ian Spencer Henry's shin so hard, he cried out in pain. "Jack!" He whimpered, and I bit back a curse, knowing the albino had caught my lie.

Only . . . he hadn't. I don't think he even heard anything after I told him we were orphans.

"Orphans." He tested the word. "Orphans, huh? Criminy, that might work. That just might work. Orphans, by my boots and socks! Yes, sir. Orphans."

He traced a calloused fingertip over the rim of the lunch pail, nodding, licking his cracked lips. "All right," he said at last. "I'll tell you the story, then we'll talk. But here's me rule. Twenty years I been after this gold, and I ain't 'bout to lose it now. So oncet I tells you this story, oncet you hears it, it don't leave your lips. Ever. I tell you this, just so you know I ain't no fool spreadin' lies. But you don't tell nobody oncet I'm done. Else I *will* cut out your hearts. But iffen you wants to join me, pardners we'll be. There's a fortune in gold coin in Doubtful Cañon, and I aims to get it. By all rights, it's mine anyways."

So he told his story. At least, part of it.

He finished the peaches, slurped down the juice, wiping his face with his dingy bandanna, then belched.

"You kids," he said, "y'all wouldn't happen to have no whiskey on you, would you?"

Feeling the stares of Ian Spencer Henry on me, I bit my lip as my face flushed. Maybe he thought

I might have brought a bottle of Pa's forty-rod to hide from him. Maybe he just feared how I would react to the albino's question.

"Rye? Tequila? Don't rightly matter as long as it's wet and bites. Anything?"

"No," Jasmine answered. "I'm eleven going on twelve. Ian Spencer Henry and Jack just turned twelve. We're too little. . . ."

He laughed. "Too li'l'? Young 'uns, I was drinkin' rye whiskey without no water chaser afore I was ten. Figgered, criminy, sneakin' off to this ol' mine for a snort, that's somethin' I'd 'a' done back when I was just a shirt tail. So. . . ."

"No whiskey," Jasmine repeated, her voice firm, face hard, demanding. "Nothing."

Until that moment, I had not realized that Jasmine and I held something else in common. We despised whiskey and those who let strong drink ruin their lives. My pa. Jasmine's fallen mother and her lynched father.

"Well. . . ." The old man sighed. "Well, that's all right. Now, the story. Where was I?"

"You were leaving the station at Stein's Peak," Ian Spencer Henry belted out. "Sam Golden and the Mex rode atop the Concord, leaving you and the gunman named Bruce and the boss man, Mister John James Giddings, inside. The Apaches had left the station in ruins, your team was tuckered out, but you had no choice but to go on. So you rode out . . . for Doubtful Cañon." Ian Spencer Henry grinned, revealing the missing front tooth, his prize, for lack of a better word, possession. "Doubtful Cañon. And death!"

Whitey Grey nodded solemnly. "You gots a good

memory, boy. I likes that in a pardner. Yeah, that's about the size of it. So, yeah, we left, rode into the Valley of the Shadow of Death, the sun sinkin' lower now in the horizon, and that's what awaited us in that mean ol' cañon of treachery and barbarity. Death."

Chapter Three

The white-skinned man picked up his tale.

Stein's Peak be the largest point in the Peloncillos, but Doubtful Cañon's the most dangerous spot in the mountains, maybe the most dangersome in this whole territory. Like I done tol' you, our mules was pret' much played out, even with the hatfuls of water Sam Golden had given 'em back at the station. They was game, though, and Sam Golden knowed he had to get us through that cañon in a hurry.

Talk about a bone-jarrin' ride, we inside that Concord was bouncin' ever' which way. I recollect hearin' some fool joke that the best way to make a good jam was to put a bunch of womenfolks in one of Mr. Butterfield's stagecoaches for the ride 'cross New Mexico.

"Hiya! Hiya! Habakkuk, Zephaniah, Haggai, and Zechariah, get movin' you blasted mules!" Sam Golden yelled from atop, and kept lashin' out with that blacksnake of his'n. *Pop! Pop*, it'd go. Sounded just like a gunshot ever' time.

Fact is, that's what I thought it was at first. *Pop!* Figgered that was Sam Golden's whip again. Only it wasn't. And then I knowed.

"Apaches!" The Mex yelled out something in Mex, and cut loose with both barrels of the shotgun.

Well, that gunfire sounded like there was a whole army of Cherry Cows, but Apaches always raided with small parties. 'Course, one Apache is often-times enough to gets the job done.

So I crouched down by one door, and Bruce, he took the other, us bouncin' up and down and 'cross, tryin' to find somethin' to shoot at, tryin' to keep still just long enough so ol' Sam wouldn't spoil our aim. Mr. Giddings, he was right behind us, a Navy Colt in his right hand, kept lookin' back at the saddlebags of money he was carryin', sworn to protect. He'd look over my shoulder, then Bruce's, all the while tryin' to balance, to keep his feet in that cascadin' stagecoach. A bullet splintered the wood not more'n an inch from my head, and I fell on my haunches, stunned, then scrambled back to my position and poked that ol' Enfield out the window. Seen 'em chargin', I did, through the thick dust Sam Golden was raisin', 'bout five of 'em murderous savages, yippin' like wolves, black hair blowin' in the wind, faces all painted for war. That'll put fear in your gut. Make a man swear off drinkin' for a month of Sundays.

We was rollin' somethin' fast, but steady now, not bouncin' so much, and I drawed me a bead on the nearest of 'em Cherry Cows. Had him dead center. Figgered on sendin' him to that happy huntin' ground.

"That's right, Sam, just keep it steady," I said, almost like I was prayin' . . . which maybe I was, I reckon . . . and right afore I pulled the trigger, we run over a rock 'bout the size of Denver City. My Enfield roared, but I knowed I'd missed. Knowed I hadn't even scairt that Apache, and I was bouncin' all the way to Bruce's side of the Concord, cussin' Sam Golden for all he was worth, half figgerin' that the coach would turn over after a jolt like that, that the mules would break their traces and we'd crash.

"Sam, you fool! We can't shoot nothin' with you drivin' like that!"

He didn't answer. Bruce chanced a couple of shots from his Navies, then ducked. Mr. Giddings fired, too. That thick white smoke burned my eyes, which has always been prone to irritation with my condition, you see.

I cussed, took back my position, and drawed one of my Navy Thirty-Sixes. We hit another rock or hole or somethin', and I jammed my hand against the door frame, like to have busted my wrist, come close to leavin' that Navy in the dust for one of 'em chargin' Injuns to pick up. I cussed Sam Golden again, cussed him loud and hard and proper. That's when I realized I didn't hear that poppin' no more. Didn't hear the Mex shootin', neither. Didn't hear nothin' from up top. Smelt smoke is all, smoke and dust and the stink of our own sweat, 'cause we was sweatin' heaps.

"Sam?" I hollered. "Sam Golden, you ain't dead, are you?" When he didn't reply, I called out the Mex's name, and Mr. Giddings took up the query, too.

"Valdez? Golden? Answer us. Do you need assistance?"

The answer we got was another bone-bustin' bump.

"Only assistance they need," I said underneath my breath, "is a merciful Lord."

Well, I shoved the Navy in my sash, and, riskin' my head and hair, I stuck myself out of the window.

Heard a bullet whistle by. Then an arrow thudded in the Concord door, slicin' my britches, and blood trickled down my thigh. But I had me a good grip on the rail up above, and pulled myself up. Hat blowed off. Wonder it'd stayed on my head this long, and 'em Apaches went to whoopin' and hollerin' like happy devils when they seen my white locks. Figured that would make a mighty good trophy hangin' from one of their acoustics. Then I grabbed another hold, pulled myself up higher, put my boots on the door.

When we bounced again, well, that was almost the death of Whitey Grey.

"Hang on!" Mr. Giddings called, but I didn't need no encouragin'. With a final lunge, I was atop the Concord.

"Mister Grey?" I heard the boss man call out. "Are you all right?"

"Yeah!" I snapped. Dust and dirt stung my eyes, and I crawled and rolled, more like fell, off the top into the driver's box.

"How are Valdez and Golden?"

"Dead!" I answered, leg startin' to pain me, and tried to find the reins.

Only, they wasn't there. No reins. No Mex. No Sam Golden.

The Mex and jehu, I figgered, had gotten 'emselves kilt, shot offen the coach. The reins was danglin' down amongst the harnesses, traces, tree, and Overland road. Then I seen a big buck of a Cherry Cow, standin' on a rock, 'bout to shoot me dead, but I whipped out one of my Navy Colts and blasted that cur. Saw the blood just a-spurtin' from his breast as he flung back into the cactus.

Arrows and bullets was flyin' ever'where, and 'em

mules was runnin' for their lives. Reckon they knowed that Apaches fancy mule meat. Sweeter it is than venison or beefsteak. Likes it my ownself. Me, I was tryin' to figger out just how I could gets control of the team. Well, then I spotted the rock. Big one. Big! And I knowed we was all goners.

I was jumpin' afore we hit, hopin' that with luck I'd just break my neck and not get caught alive by 'em Cherry Cows. Landed hard, and heard the crashin', the screamin' of the mules, figgered Bruce and Mr. Giddings was dead, too. My lip was busted, had lost two good teeth, and I knowed my right ankle was broke, but I was still breathin', and I rolled over, pulled myself to my feet, saw the Concord there on its side, the mules runnin' down the cañon. I spat out blood, reached for one Navy, but I'd lost it in my tumble, so I jerked the other free, and limped toward the wagon. Those Apaches was right behind us. The door on the top flung open, knockin' off a few arrows, and then I spied Mr. Giddings's bell crown hat. He tossed up his saddlebags afore he crawled out atop. An arrow knocked off his hat, and he pivoted like a gunman and fired two quick shots.

Game as a bantam rooster, he was. He tossed off 'em there bags, and turned 'round, helpin' Bruce out of the Concord.

Well, I run faster, fast as I could, ankle busted like it was, and my leg still bleedin' and smartin' from that arrow wound. Takin' up me a position by the busted wagon tongue, I eyed the Apaches and shot one of the horses dead, spillin' the rider. Hope that Cherry Cow busted his neck.

That took a little starch out of 'em Apaches. They figured this fight was all over, but we showed 'em we wasn't quittin'. Couldn't quit. Not amongst 'em red devils. Mr. Giddings hopped down beside me, carryin' those heavy saddlebags on his shoulders, pistol in his right hand. He didn't look too banged up considerin' the spill he had taken in that coach. Should've broked his neck.

But, Bruce, now, he didn't fare so well. White bone was stickin' out of his right forearm, and his face was covered with blood. Big gash on his forehead, nose smashed to a pulp. Didn't have none of his guns, neither.

I figgered he wouldn't be long for this world, but don't reckon I guessed he'd die that quick. What happened was, afore I could say a thing or draw a breath, a Cherry Cow arrow pierced his throat, right underneath his Adam's apple, from one side to the other. Just like that. We was just starin' at each other, wonderin' how we was still alive, and then that hired killer was gaggin', chokin' on his own blood, eyes bulgin' out of their sockets, and afore it even struck us what had happened, he had sunk to his knees and leaned against the stagecoach and just up and died.

Mr. Giddings and I found us a better hidin' spot, and then I spied my Enfield. Stock was busted, and it bein' a singleshot, which I had done fired, it wasn't good for a fightin' weapon no more, but I sure needed some help walkin', so I picked it up to use as a crutch.

"We're dead. There's no escape, no hope, but we cannot let this gold fall into the Apaches' hands," Mr. Giddings said.

"Hold on there!" I called out, but Mr. Giddings just took off runnin' toward the rocks, the weight of that gold slowin' him down, causin' him to stagger and weave. "Come back here, you fool!" Bullets kicked up dust at his feet, but he made it to the ca-ñon's edge, disappearin' in the rocks. I spotted black hair and a blue headband just above where he had vanished, knowed it was an Apache, and fired two shots with my Navy.

Now, I couldn't keep up with Mr. Giddings, not with my ankle busted, and I reckon I had me as good a spot to die as any right there by the stage. Had water, a little food, another cylinder, capped and loaded, for my Thirty-Six in my possibles bag, and my fallen comrade, ol' Bruce from Wisconsin way, for comp'ny. I looked at the sun, then toward where I had last seen Mr. Giddings, and, with a sigh, I just leaned against the coach and sank down to a seated position, proppin' up the busted Enfield be-side me.

The wheel was spinnin' overhead, squeakin', and afore too many seconds had passed, I realized that was the only sound I heard. Nothin'. Deadly quiet. I spat out some more salty blood, checked my Navy Colt, wondered if I should just kill myself now and be done with it. No use in waitin' for the Apaches to attack, 'cause they would, soon enough.

It's funny what'll go through a man's mind when he's that close to dyin'. Well, no point in gettin' to all that, now. So there I sat, waitin' to die, figgered Mr. Giddings was dead by now, and next thing I knowed, I seen him. His head popped up from the rocks, next his whole body, 'em saddlebags gone, but the six-shooter still in his hand. First, I taken it for a mi-rage, maybe some apparition, but I never heard of no mirage talkin'.

"Mister Grey?" he yelled.

Well, I was just too stunned to answer. I lifted my Colt a wee bit, tried to wave him back, but he must have figured I was bad hurt, so, brave man that he was, he come chargin' back. I won't forget that. Won't forget what a gallant man he was.

Fool, though. Just a fool thing to do. Should have stayed in the rocks. Might have made it out of that scrap alive, but he was comin' toward me. Comin' to save me.

The first arrow hit him in the back of his left leg, right in the bend of the knee, and he fell. He was rollin' over when a bullet shattered his left arm. I saw the Apache, the one I had seen afore and shot at, rise up, an old Sharps in his hands, grinnin' like he'd just drawed to an inside straight, and started to fire that big ol' buffalo gun, but Mr. Giddings beat me and him to it. He put two bullets in that Cherry Cow's belly afore that Injun knowed what had happened.

Well, I was thinkin', *he took one of 'em vermin with 'im.*

But that was it. Arrows flied out from all over like a covey of quail, pinnin' Mr. Giddings to the ground.

I just sank back down, almost cried, I did, but then I shook some sense into me. Scairt as I was, bad hurt as I was, I wasn't 'bout to shame Mr. John James Giddings's memory by bawlin' like some yellow-livered coward. No, sir. I could die as game as he could.

So I cocked that Navy of mine, and waited for 'em Apaches to come finish the job.

Chapter Four

"So, how'd you get away?"

The question escaped my mouth before I realized I had even spoken. I'd even beaten Ian Spencer Henry to it, and I rarely got a word in edgewise with my best friend nearby.

"Directly, sonny, directly," the white-faced man answered without looking at me. He belched, a foul, bean-smelling burp that stunk up the mine's entrance more than when he broke wind earlier. Next, Whitey Grey fished out paper and tobacco sack and began rolling a cigarette, but his makings were so old and dry, his first two attempts fell into ruin, while Jasmine, Ian Spencer Henry, and I waited eagerly, anxiously, wondering if he would ever finish his blood-and-thunder story.

At last, the third cigarette survived the ordeal, and he stuck the smoke in his mouth, then patted down his pockets for a Lucifer. To our relief, the cigarette flared up much quicker than it had taken him to roll it, and he leaned back, pulling hard, savoring the taste and smell of tobacco—personally, I preferred the sulphuric aroma of the stricken match over that of cigarette smoke.

There we sat, as if in some trance.

"Night come on me," he said at last, only, just as soon as he had resurrected his story, he departed on yet another detour. "Young 'uns, you sure you ain't gots no whiskey on you or gots a bottle hidden somewhere close by? 'Tain't nothin' like a mornin' bracer on top of Caroliny-cured tobaccy."

"We don't have anything," Ian Spencer Henry said, "but there are eleven dram shops and dance halls on Avon Avenue alone, Mister Grey." My friend smiled in a triumphant brag. "I've counted them."

Whitey Grey nodded without much appreciation. "Well, don't matter none. Where was I again, chil'ren?"

This time, Jasmine spoke first, reminding this stranger of where he had left off, and he repeated that darkness had fallen on him at Doubtful Cañon on that April day two decades earlier.

"Apaches be scairt of the dark," he said. "Y'all ain't afeared of no hobgoblins or haunts in the night, is you?"

Shakes of our heads reassured him, or, maybe, tried to convince us of our own bravery.

"Good, good. But 'em Cherry Cows won't never attack after dark. Odd creatures, 'em Apache. Fearless in the daylight, but, oncet that sun sets, they ain't prone to fightin'. Scairt if they gets kilt, they'll never find their way to the happy land, or if they kill someone, maybe that dead fella's ghost won't be able to find his way to the happy land and will follow his slayer for the rest of his days. Or somethin' like that. I ain't claimin' to know all there is to know about no Apache. No, sir. They be hard to savvy. Most Injuns is that way. But, point is, Cherry Cows just won't keep up no attack come dark."

When he paused his story for another drag on his

smoke, I took advantage of the opening to ask a question that had plagued me since his story began. "Apaches don't take scalps, either," I informed Whitey Grey. "But you kept saying they'd lift your hair . . . things like that. Could you explain?"

Whitey Grey's cold, dead eyes flamed with anger as he flicked the cigarette into dark corner.

"You callin' me a liar, boy?"

"No, sir. . . ." A dread filled my stomach, and I felt sick, maybe scared, and a sharp pain suddenly raced up my leg and down my foot. Ian Spencer Henry had paid me back, had kicked me in the ankle for talking too much.

My friend gave me his own angry stare, but, when I looked back toward Whitey Grey, I saw the full extent of the albino's rage, reflecting in those hollow eyes. Chilled? Petrified? I'm not sure I have a word in my vocabulary that will do justice to the fear I felt at that moment. I can't say my young life passed before my eyes, as that tired saying goes, but I did find myself choking down fright, or, at least, trying to. The dread kept rising till I could almost taste it, and then Whitey Grey broke out in a roar of laughter that echoed into the nethermost, midnight-black depths of the Lady Macbeth Mine until it sounded as if a chorus of demons were laughing with him.

He reached over and patted my trembling knee with a hard, calloused hand, then gave my two friends reassuring pats.

"You got a curious, suspicious mind, don't you . . . what's that you say your name is?"

"Jack," I answered. "Jack Dunivan."

"Yeah, yeah, Jack Dunivan. That's right. Jack Dunivan, Ian Spencer Henry, and Jasmine Allison. My pardners." At that instant, he slammed his palms together in a thunderous clap. Whitey Grey grinned. "Bully for you, Master Jack Dunivan, 'cause this old hoss here, Whitey Grey, he likes a curious, suspicious man for his pardner. 'Specially if he's gotta trust that pardner in as treacherous a place as 'em Peloncillo Mountains. That's because 'em Cherry Cows may be cooped up on the San Carlos Reservation over in Arizony now, but, well, that desert country that I be bound for is knowed for bein' filled with other right mean folk. Mexican bandits. White men like 'em Clantons from Tombstone way. Rustlers, thieves, bushwhackers, and murderers. A fellow had better have a suspicious nature iffen he wants to live long in that country." With another smile, he patted Jasmine's leg. "A girlie fellow had better be suspicious, too."

"I am," she reassured him. "And Jack's right. Apaches don't scalp. Papa told me. . . ." Her eyes fell down, and she pulled up her legs, wrapping her arms tightly around the knees, and closed her eyes, remembering, I guess, or maybe trying to forget.

"How long you kids been in Shakespeare?" he asked.

We answered meekly, all except Jasmine, who kept silent, her eyes shut tightly, rocking back and forth and biting her upper lip.

It occurred to me that Whitey Grey had not answered the question I had posed, and I began to think of him as a liar, one of those miners full of braggadocio, or, another word I'd heard Mr. Shankin say when the mercantile owner was not around polite company.

Maybe the albino had read my mind, or face, for he began nodding and leaned back on his throne. "I first come through Apache territory when I weren't much older than you tots. Diff'rent country back then . . . like I done tol' you I don't recollect how many times. And, Master Jack Dunivan, you be right. You, too, li'l' girlie. Apaches wasn't prone to takin' a scalp back then. Most of 'em won't do it now, but some of 'em learnt from their wicked red vermin brothers."

"Wicked white men, too." Jasmine came full alert. "Mexicans and Americans have paid bounties for Apache scalps!"

"Don't turn renegade on me, li'l' girlie. Ain't nothin' ol' Whitey Grey despises more than some Injun lover. Had you seen what 'em bad boys done to those folks at that stage station, seen how they cut down that gallant Mister Giddings, him with his best years left to live, you wouldn't feel sorry for no dead Apache. Me? I taken me a few Apache scalps my own self and consider that bounty money well earned and well spent." Another crooked, mirthless smile. "But, sure, sure, even Cherry Cows don't care much for liftin' hair, but they do other things that'd make a Comanch' look like the biggest God-fearin' sky pilot you ever laid your eyes on. Yeah, I knowed most Apaches don't take scalps. Just a sayin' mostly, young 'uns. You gots to remember that I growed up in Texas. And I seen many a white family missin' their topknots from Comanche and Kiowa knifes. Even some Apache."

His explanation quieted my suspicions, although I imagine he could have said anything and I would have believed him, so strong burned my desire to find a reason to escape Shakespeare and my father, the cemetery, and my shame.

"Luck." Whitey Grey let out a long, sad sigh. His opaque eyes dropped, and for what seemed like minutes, though could have lasted only a few seconds, he seemingly stared at his battered, dusty mismatched boots. We waited, holding our breaths, as the white-skinned man's head bobbed as if answering some silent question he had posed himself. "That's what it was," he said, looking up. "Nothin' more'n luck. Oncet the sun set, things turned real quiet, even quieter than they had been right after that brave man got slaughtered right afore my eyes. It was over, for now, and I figured that this be my only chance. So shovin' my Navy in my sash, I used that ol' busted up Enfield of mine as a crutch, and I just walked, well, hobbled over to the far wall past Mister Giddings's body. Carried one canteen with me. Then I just hugged real close to the cañon wall and eased my way eastward. That was the gamble, but I decided that oncet them bucks realized I had flowed the coop, they'd guess than I walked west, toward the San Simon and into that peaceful valley. Nothin' back at Stein's Peak station but a poisoned well and dead men and ruins. And you gots to recollect that most of 'em Apaches was between me and Stein's Peak. But I limped out of there east, real careful-like. Because while it's a knowed fact that Cherry Cows won't attack nobody at night, I highly suspected that if some crippled up, starvin', thirsty pale eyes was to stumble right into their camp, they'd swarm on me like flies on grizzly scat, yes, sir, knives and war clubs workin'. That's what I done. I walked. Walked right past 'em and on toward that burnt out shell of a station.

Fooled 'em, I did. Fooled 'em good. Took me a long time to cover only a few miles, but, come sunup, I was back at Stein's Peak. Just collapsed against the tumblin' walls. I guess I still expected the Cherry Cows to come back and finish the job, but for some reason they didn't. A body can't figure no Apache, that's the truth. I don't reckon I moved hardly a muscle all that day and into the next. Plumb tuckered out I was. Drank what was left in the canteen I had, but I didn't have nothin' to eat, not that my ol' stomach could hold nothin'. Might've been slightly touched in the head by the sun, by all that I'd been through, but I was just sittin' there, breathin', when some boys' drivin' freight wagons come through. Must 'a' been the next day, I guess. To be honest, I ain't quite sure, but they come, give me some whiskey, took me into the back of one of their wagons. They say I was talkin' clear out of my head, but, after they give me more whiskey and some coffee and just a li'l' bit of soup and bacon, I come back to bein' my old self. Tol' 'em what had happened, and we went on westward. The freighters had a strong supply of muskets, and was ready for any attack, but we never seen no more Apaches. Redskins just disappeared, which is also their nature. We did come across the bodies of poor Sam Golden and the Mex. Picked to pieces, they'd been. Not by the Apaches, mind you, but other vermin . . . wolves and coyotes and ravens and vultures. Nothin' left of 'em but their bones and some rags of clothin'. Buried 'em where we found 'em. Found the wrecked Concord coach just where it'd been left, too, shot to pieces, plundered. And, of course, more bones. All that was left of Bruce and the valiant Mister Giddings. We laid 'em to rest, too. And we lit a shuck out of Doubtful Cañon. I stuck with the wagon train till we reached Tucson, reported the missin' gold and all that had happened to the superintendent of the Overland Mail there. And that was it.

"You left the gold?" Ian Spencer Henry asked in disbelief. "Why didn't you stay after you had buried those men? Why not look for it then?"

The albino dismissed the twelve-year-old's question with a snort. "In Doubtful Cañon? After Apaches had just slaughtered dozens of men?"

Ever the mathematician, my friend corrected Whitey Grey's number, and Jasmine pointed out that the Apaches had vanished. The albino snorted and shook his head.

"Yeah, 'em Cherry Cows had vamoosed, but that don't mean they wasn't 'bout to come back and kill the rest of us. Apaches can vanish, but they been knowed to un-vanish, too. 'Sides, those boys who had saved my bacon wasn't interested in money, even had I tol' 'em 'bout it. All they wanted was to get out of that deadly place in one piece. So did I. No, sir, I didn't tell 'em 'bout the treasure we was packin' in that stage. Didn't tell nobody . . . wasn't rightly sure I could trust 'em, you see . . . till I met with the boss man in Tucson."

He grinned, and leaned toward us, lowering his voice to a whisper. "But I'm trustin' you three young 'uns. You be my pardners, bein' orphans and all. You chil'ren game?"

Chapter Five

For a moment, no one spoke. Whitey Grey didn't even blink, just glared, waiting. My first glance fell upon Ian Spencer Henry, who wet his lips, hopeful but anxious; next, I turned toward Jasmine Allison, who stared at me with her pretty, pleading dark eyes. Neither wanted to cast a vote, and they looked at me as the leader, a rank I desired not.

"When do . . . ?" I had to clear my throat to make myself heard as I faced Whitey Grey. "When do you need an answer?"

The albino frowned. "Chil'ren," he said, "I offered y'all five thousand dollars. That's practically two thousand each for orphans barely knee-high to a sidewinder. It's. . . ."

"Sixteen hundred," Ian Spencer Henry interrupted.

"What's that?" said Whitey Grey, dumbfounded.

"Sixteen hundred," my friend repeated, "and sixty-six dollars. Not two thousand. And sixty-seven cents." He grinned. "I did that in my head. One thousand six hundred sixty-six dollars and sixty-seven cents. Of course, one of us will get one less penny because of the division. Three's not an even number, you see."

"Yeah, I see." But, of course, the white-skinned man saw nothing. "I'm lightin' a shuck for that treasure at ten o' the clock tonight. Take us an hour or so to get to the Southern Pacific, where we'll board the train and ride to Stein's. Y'all want to join me, y'all come here right afore that time. And don't tarry 'cause we gots to catch that westbound. But I wants all three of you. I ain't one to leave no young 'un behind and have him, or her, spill my story and have ever' high-grader and bushwhacker between Tombstone and Mesilla chasin' my gold. Y'all savvy that?"

Our heads bobbed.

"It's a right smart of money I've offered to share," the stranger continued. "I been generous, as be my nature. But if a one of you tells anybody, even the nearest priest, I'll figger you done betrayed me, and I slits the throats of those who try to cheat Whitey Grey."

With that, he stood. "Ten tonight. All of you, or none of you."

He moved with surprisingly quickness through the Lady Macbeth's entrance, turned the corner, and vanished.

Ian Spencer Henry rose, peeked around the corner, and, with a shrug, turned to me. "I figure we'd give Jasmine two extra cents," he said.

"What?" I asked.

"If we go. Instead of one of us getting only sixty-six cents, I figured you and I would give up a penny. Sixteen hundred and sixty-six dollars and sixty-six cents for you and me, Jack, but Jasmine gets sixty-eight cents. I did that in my head, too."

"I'm not sure any of us will get any money." Rising slowly, I tested the ankle Ian Spencer Henry had kicked.

"You don't believe his story?" Jasmine leaned forward, gathering the remnants and trash from the albino's meal.

"I have some investigating to do," I explained and started to leave the mine.

"But I want to go!" Jasmine cried out. "Don't stop us."

"Yeah," Ian Spencer Henry said. "You'll ruin everything, Jack. Get our throats cut or something. That ghostly man is right. Sixteen hundred dollars, that's more money than we'll ever see around here."

I whirled back toward my friends. "Why does he want three kids with him?" That question had troubled me since hearing the albino's proposition.

"Because," my two comrades sang out in unison.

"Because why?"

"Because . . . is all." Ian Spencer Henry stared at his feet. Arithmetic problems he could solve with ease, but this proved a different type of equation.

"Likely, he thinks he can cheat us," Jasmine said after a moment's reflection. "And for some reason, he needs us."

"Nobody needs a twelve-year-old," I said, and thought of my father. Plagued by doubt. That kept proving to be my undoing, the way I saw things. Earlier, I had been so mesmerized by the stranger's story, I would have done anything to believe him, would have gone with him in an instant, but now he was gone, and with it had departed my resolve to follow him. Perhaps some form of sanity, or reason, had rooted itself in me.

"You're a 'fraidy cat," Ian Spencer Henry taunted.

"Yeah," Jasmine agreed, both of them sounding like the children they were. The children *we* were.

I let out a long sigh, peered around the corner to

make sure Whitey Grey had indeed gone, and shook my head. "No, I'm not. I want to go more than any of you, but I'm not going into that desert blind. I just think things through is all. You know that, the both of you. You want to get left behind in Doubtful Cañon? You want to die of thirst? Killed by bandits? And have you thought about how we can explain our disappearance? We can't just walk out of here with that man." I jabbed a finger at Ian Spencer Henry's chest. "Your pa will come looking for you!"

He snorted and spat in contempt. "My pa still thinks I'm attending the subscription school, Jack. He don't know nothing except rocks and figures."

"Doesn't know anything," I corrected, ever the teacher.

"And my ma doesn't care a fip for me. She's too busy." Jasmine put both hands on her hips, glaring, daring.

"And your pa. . . ." Ian Spencer Henry stopped, and studied his shoes again.

My stomach roiled. I felt my body tremble.

"Sorry, Jack," my best friend whispered when he finally looked up.

"It's just a way out, Jack," Jasmine said. "Please. . . ."

Somewhere outside, a dog barked and a cat snarled. I fought to regain my composure, and, without looking at my friends, I said: "I just want to make sure everything is all right. I want to get out of here, get away from this place more than you know. But. . . . Let's meet back here before supper. I'll let you know then."

It's hard to find a man you can trust in Shakespeare.

Mr. Shankin had said that to my father before our

family tragedy—although I can't place the context of that conversation—back when Pa had been saving money to open his newspaper shop. I always remembered those words, especially once the bottle laid Pa low, and, whenever I found a troublesome puzzle, I sought out the mercantile owner. He had proved to be the father, the teacher, I had lost.

Never had Shakespeare lured a population of philanthropists. When miners first found silver ore in the nearby hills back around 1870, the mining camp went by the name Ralston, after some California banker. Ralston's men controlled the camp, controlled the stagecoaches, and just about every business in town. More miners flocked to the desert, searching for their own mother lode, but Ralston's backers had hired a vigilance committee made up of Texians, and these gunmen—The Hired Fighting Men—pretty much kept the newcomers from making any claims, at least, good claims. The first veins played out quickly, but before Ralston could die, stories sprang up about diamonds being discovered at Lee's Peak. So Ralston, and The Hired Fighting Men, survived for a few more months—until revelations that the diamond mines were a hoax, nothing more, just a way for Ralston's men to pluck more money from the pokes of honest miners.

Upon discovery of that deceit, the Ralston men fled back to California, Texas, and points unknown, and the mining camp quickly died until the second legitimate silver strike drew more fortune-seekers to the desert, and brought a new name, Shakespeare, to the settlement.

Those Hired Fighting Men—couldn't the vigilantes have come up with a better name than that?—had been Texians, and it would not have surprised me to learn that Whitey Grey had been one of those scoundrels. I merely suspected this, but wanted to learn from Mr. Shankin if he had ever heard of Whitey Grey or a stagecoach being attacked by Apaches in Doubtful Cañon back in 1861.

I found him busy with two gentleman customers when I darted through the door. Not miners, not the way they dressed, a stark contrast to the soiled, mismatched duds Whitey Grey donned. One man stood, chewing on a peppermint stick like a cigar, with striped britches stuck into handsome boots equipped with musical, big-rowel spurs, and a blue shield-front shirt trimmed in yellow piping with a flowery B stitched in the center of the bib. He twirled a black Stetson in his left hand while his right rested on the ivory handle of a .44 Russian that rested butt forward in a dark holster on his left hip.

This man I remembered. It hadn't been that long ago that I'd seen Curly Bill Brocious use that revolver on a cardsharp not far from here.

The second man, also dark-haired, although his lacked the waves of Brocious's locks, sat in his stocking feet, the legs of his gray trousers pulled up to his knees. He twiddled his thumbs, waiting patiently for Mr. Shankin to bring over a pair of fancy tan boots with long mule-ear pulls. His black hat had been pushed back, and he wore a red, billowy shirt, black cravat, and a fine waistcoat that matched his pants. His shell belt held two holsters, something I'd never seen except on the covers of the half-dime novels Mr. Shankin and Ian Spencer Henry peddled. From the way the revolver butts faced, I assumed this man to be left-handed.

"Hello, Jack," Mr. Shankin greeted me warmly. "How are you faring today?" Before I could answer, he placed the boots beside the two-gun man's feet. "Try these on, sir," he told his customer and looked back at me. "You need anything, son?"

"I can come back." I started to go.

"No need to run off, kid. It'll take Dutch here half the day to get them boots over his stinkin' socks." The last time I'd heard that voice, Brocious had been screaming at those Mexicans to bury the gambler he had killed.

"What do you need, Jack?" Mr. Shankin asked kindly.

"Just wondering." Slowly I turned back around. "It's nothing important."

The first boot went on with a grunt, and Brocious slammed the hat on his head, grabbing the candy with his free hand as his teeth crunched the stick in half. The second man pulled his left boot on with a soft *whoosh*, and rose slowly, then walked to the far end of the store, testing the new footwear.

"What's on your mind, Jack?" Mr. Shankin asked again.

With Brocious chomping on his candy and the other gunman testing out the new pair of boots, I asked the mercantile owner if he had ever heard of Apaches attacking a stagecoach in Doubtful Cañon back in 1861.

"Jack Dunivan here is bound to be a newspaper editor," Mr. Shankin told Brocious with a beaming smile. "He's. . . ." He never finished, likely remembering my father's troubles, and looked away from me, asking Brocious's pal how the boots fit.

"Kind of big," the man said in a quiet voice.

"Pour some water in them," Brocious said. "Walk around with them wet all day. Leather'll shrink. Fit fine after that bit of doctoring."

"I'm not one to waste water like that, Curly."

Shrugging, Brocious wiped sticky fingers on his bib front. "Well, buy them or take them off. We need to ride soon."

"That's the only size I have in that style, sir," Mr. Shankin said. "I could order you a pair, but that would take at least six or eight weeks."

"No cobbler in Shakespeare?" the man asked.

"No, sir."

"Well, let me walk around a minute more. I do like the way they look, and the fit isn't that bad."

"The water treatment does work," Mr. Shankin said.

As the gunman walked back toward the bolts of cotton, Mr. Shankin turned back toward me. "That's a little before my time, Jack, to answer your inquiry," he said. "Back in 'Sixty-One I hung my hat in Terre Haute before joining the Thirty-Second Regiment to save the Union. Yet I have heard of many dreadful things happening in Doubtful Cañon. You might ask John Eversen. He re-opened the stage station after the rebellion when the Kerens and Mitchell Company ran stages from San Diego. Granted, I don't think John ever worked the Butterfield lines, but if anyone remembers about the time you ask about, it would be him."

"Thank you, sir. I'll do that." I paused, wondering if I should ask a second question, then glanced outside to make sure the albino was nowhere in sight. Summoning up the courage, I asked if he had ever heard of a man named Whitey Grey.

Crunch!

I spun, my heart racing, only to see Curly Bill Brocious had helped himself to a second piece of stick candy. Grinning, he picked a morsel of candy from his waxed mustache and flicked it on the floor.

"That's not a name I recall," Mr. Shankin answered. "I can ask around. . . ."

"No," I said, louder than I meant. "Don't do that. It's nothing important, just a story Ian Spencer Henry was telling me and. . . ."

The merchant laughed. "I wouldn't put much stock in any story that young man tells you, Jack. Probably something he read that Ned Buntline dreamed up."

"Yes, sir. Thank you." Turning to go, I stepped into the sunlight, thinking I had made up my mind.

A voice stopped me. "Doubtful Cañon's no place to be." I looked back inside to see the second man staring at me. His eyes seemed almost hollow, a cold blue, and his smile held little warmth. It felt like he had issued me a warning.

"That's certain," Mr. Shankin added. "Half the time, I don't think New Mexico's any place to be. I'm just glad the Army ran off Nana and his Red Paint Apaches."

"Yeah," the cold-eyed man said, still staring at me.

In July and August, Nana and a small party of Apaches had cut across southern New Mexico, attacking the Army, ranches, even towns, although they stayed clear of Shakespeare. By the middle of August, Nana's raiders had crossed into Sonora and disappeared. Peace, always tenuous, had come again to New Mexico.

Dismissing me, the stranger pointed at the boots and told the mercantile owner: "Reckon I'll take these."

Doubtful Cañon was no place to be. I felt certain of that. I didn't need to look up old John Eversen, for I had practically made up my mind that I would not be joining Whitey Grey. A disappointment, certainly, shattering my dreams of escape. Yet the man couldn't be trusted, and I doubted his story, doubted everything he had told us. At that moment, he probably sat in some bucket of blood on Avon Avenue laughing at the stretcher he had told three children. He'd be sniggering, if sober, come ten o'clock that night, wondering how many fool children had returned to an empty mine.

A shout across the street drew my attention, and I turned and froze, watching the bouncer at Falstaff's Tavern wipe his meaty paws on his apron before pointing a thick finger at the drunk he had just pitched into the street. "I told you to stay out of this place. Show your mug again, and I'll break more than that nose." Someone inside the saloon handed him a plug hat, which he tossed nonchalantly into the street before returning to his post.

The drunk picked himself up, grabbed the hat, and pulled it on his head, then swayed, cursing the swinging batwing doors. "I don't need you," he said, pivoted, and leaned against a hitching rail, shaking his head and testing his busted nose. His eyes caught me and held, or so I thought, and then he wobbled across the street, dodging a buckboard with an oath, and drew nearer.

"Mister," he said in a thick slur, "could you loan an old hand enough money for a drink or two. I got me a powerful thirst."

My face reddened, and I trembled again. My father, my wretched father stood there so in his cups, he didn't even recognize his own son. Blood trickled from both nostrils into his thick scruff of beard, unkempt, unwashed. "I can do you some turn," he said. "Water your horse. Shine them new boots."

A snort sounded behind me, and I realized my mistake. My father had directed his conversation at the two men now standing behind me, Curly Bill Brocious, still working on the peppermint, and the second man, rolling a cigar in his mouth.

"Pay the cur." The gunman called Dutch struck a match and lit his cigar. "It'll keep him off the street. Out of our sight."

With a rough laugh, Brocious fished a coin from his trouser pocket and tossed it into the dirt. "Whatever you say, Dutch. Whatever you say."

The chimes of Brocious's spurs faded as the two gunmen walked down the sun-warped boardwalk, and I stared, sickened by the sight of my father, on his knees, digging through the dirt in search of the two-bit piece Curly Bill Brocious had thrown at him.

I left him there, ashamed, hurrying to find the home of old John Eversen. Not that I needed to hear anything the old stagecoach man had to say about Doubtful Cañon, Apache attacks, and a strange man called Whitey Grey. Overruling doubts and distrust, the sight of my father had all but changed my mind, yet again, reconfirmed my desire, my need, to get away from this place. I didn't care if Whitey Grey lied or not, and, even if he didn't plan on showing up that night at the Lady Macbeth, I'd be on my way.

I was leaving.

Chapter Six

Candlelight flickered, casting a low, warm glow on my friends' faces just inside the mine's entrance. We had met, as arranged, after supper, sneaking out of our houses without incident. The desert night had turned chilly, the early autumn wind moaning outside, but the Lady Macbeth remained warm. I lit another candle, placed it on a rusty old lunch pail, and looked at my friends, their faces eager yet anxious.

"A lot of things that man says, I find suspect," I told them. "Some of what he says about Cochise and that time doesn't exactly match with what I read in some old newspapers that my father has saved. And I asked this old stagecoach man . . . Mister Shankin sent me to him . . . this afternoon. Mister Eversen never heard of a Whitey Grey. Nor has Mister Shankin."

Ian Spencer Henry gasped. "You wasn't supposed to tell nobody about that white-skinned man, Jack Dunivan. Now you done spoilt everything."

"I've done no such thing. . . ."

"Done, too!"

"Done not. I'm just collecting facts."

"No, you ruint. . . ."

"Shut up, Ian Spencer Henry," Jasmine sang out, "and let Jack finish!"

Pouting, my friend folded his arms and shook his head.

I sighed. "I'm going with Whitey Grey," I said, and Ian Spencer Henry's face beamed instantly.

"Really?" both of my friends asked, unable to control their excitement.

"Yes. But we can't trust him. That's what I'm saying."

"Well, yeah," Ian Spencer Henry said. "He's a Texian. Texians can't be trusted. I heard this fella outside the Falstaff Tavern the other day, and he says if he was standing on his porch with a single-shot shotgun and there was a rattlesnake coiled up in front of him and a Texian coming over to shake his hand, this fellow says he'd shoot the Texian and let the snake bite him."

I tried to ignore the pointless interruption. "Mister Eversen, he says that he had heard stories about Apaches raiding the Stein's Peak station right before the rebellion and an attack on a stagecoach at Doubtful Cañon, so that part of the story could be true. Plus, the Giddings name rang a bell, he told me. Seems he heard it more recent, but he couldn't place when or where. So I say we meet back here at ten. I mean, that's my plan anyway."

"Mine, too," Ian Spencer Henry said.

"Why not wait?" Jasmine asked.

"Too risky. If your mother, my pa, or Ian Spencer Henry's daddy were to check on us. . . ." Outside, coyotes began yipping in the dark. "We also need to leave a note for them to find."

"We don't want them looking for us," Ian Spencer Henry said. "What if . . . ?"

"They're going to come looking for us," I said. "They'll realize we're missing at some point. Even my. . . ." I fought off the shudder. "Well, Mister Shankin . . . someone, at some point . . . they'll realize we're not around and. . . ."

"Maybe they'll think Apaches took us off," Ian Spencer Henry suggested.

"The Apaches are all penned up at the San Carlos Reservation over in Arizona Territory," I said. "Except for maybe five hundred or so down in Mexico. We don't want to leave notes in our rooms, nothing like that. We have to make it hard for them to find us. First, they'll start looking around town. That'll give us time. But eventually they need to find a note saying that we're running away from home."

Ian Spencer Henry frowned again. "I don't want to run away from home, Jack. I just want to make all that money, sixteen hundred dollars and sixty-six cents, and get back before my pa knows I'm gone. Pa'll switch my hide if he thinks I've run off."

"It's better than twenty miles to Stein's Peak," I said. "Through desert, mean country. Then we have to make it to the cañon, find the gold, split it up, and get back here." *You get back here*, I thought. I had no intention of returning, but this wasn't the time to tell my friends of my plans for after we got our share of the treasure. "I'm pretty certain they'll find out we're missing before."

"But you've asked everyone about Doubtful Cañon," Jasmine said. "That'll be the first place they'll look."

"First, they'll look through town," I said. "And at some point they'll look here. That's where they'll find the note."

"Say we've gone to Mexico to live with *señoritas*

and drink tequila and ride horses and join some *rancho* and become *vaqueros*," Ian Spencer Henry said. "I always wanted to wear them fancy britches that them Mexican cowboys wear. I seen a good drawing on the covers of some of those fun books I so enjoy reading. Then my pa will go looking for me down south, if he thinks I've really gone, and I'm not altogether certain, Jack, that he'll ever notice I'm missing. But if he does, I think the note should say we've gone to Mexico to run off. That'll send them searching in the opposite direction of where we're going."

"They'd never believe that," Jasmine said. "They'll remember all Jack has asked about Doubtful Cañon and Stein's Peak. Ian Spencer Henry is right, Jack. You shouldn't have asked all those questions. That'll give us all away."

I drew in a deep breath, exhaled slowly, and shook my head. "I had to ask, guys," I said. "I had to find out that this fellow isn't trying to hoodwink us or something. I mean, I had to at least try. But when they look in this mine . . . because, face it, someone in Shakespeare knows this is our hide-out . . . then they'll find a note, but it's a note to fool the grown-ups. It's a note I've written to Jasmine, saying to meet us at the station at the Southern Pacific tracks."

"But, Jack," Ian Spencer Henry said, "that's where that white-skinned man says we're going. That's exactly where we're going."

"I know that," I said with not a little impatience. "But if people are looking for us, they'll likely have a tracker who'll be able to follow our trail north of here. But if you two will let me finish. This note, this letter to Jasmine, it says that I think I've fooled every-one into believing I'm interested in Doubtful Cañon and that's where they will be looking while we take the first eastbound train to El Paso. And from there to San Antonio, Texas."

They let my plan sink in. I thought it was a good one, and found their questions and doubts annoying.

"But, Jack," Ian Spencer Henry said, "there's no buried gold in San Antonio that I know of."

Jasmine broke out giggling, while I just shook my head. "We're not going to Texas! That's just so they'll look for us in Texas."

"I'd like to go to San Antonio," Ian Spencer Henry said. "See the Alamo and Texian cowboys, even though that man at the saloon said you can't trust a Texian."

"With your share, Ian Spencer Henry, with sixteen hundred dollars, I'm sure you can ride the rails to the Alamo."

"One thousand, six hundred dollars, and sixty-six cents, Jack," he said, grinning. "Because we decided to let Jasmine have an extra penny from each of us. Remember?"

I smiled back. "I remember." I blew out one candle. "Remember, we have to meet back here before ten o'clock."

After putting out the other candles, we stepped into the wind, heading back to our homes, while I wondered if Whitey Grey would show up that night, and, if he didn't, if he proved to be merely a grafter or some strange jester, what I'd do next to escape Shakespeare.

He was there, of course, when I stepped back inside the Lady Macbeth three hours later, sitting in the darkness, his cigarette glowing when he inhaled.

The small red glow seemed to cast just enough light to illuminate his deathly pale skin, although that had to be mere imagination from the mind of a frightened kid.

I cleared my throat. "Mister Grey," I said. "It's me, Jack Dunivan."

"Jack!" The voice came to my left, and I looked into the blackness.

"Jasmine?"

"Yeah. I got here first. Where's Ian Spencer Henry?"

"He'll be along directly, I suspect. Here, I got a candle. Let me. . . ."

"You ain't lightin' nothin', Jack Dunivan," Whitey Grey said. "What kept you?"

"Nothing kept me. I'm here. I'm ready. . . ."

"Looks like the li'l' girlie gots the most gumption amongst you chil'ren." The albino cackled. "That'll do. That'll do."

The glow disappeared, then I heard his boot heel crushing the butt in the dirt.

Silence. It lasted I don't know how long, and I felt my way through the void and slowly squatted. I couldn't hear a thing, not even my heart beating, not even Jasmine's breaths, nothing. Even the wind had stopped. The sounds from Shakespeare died, the dram shops and gambling parlors falling mute. Again, this must have been my imagination, or maybe I simply concentrated on listening for Ian Spencer Henry.

Yet he never came.

"Ten o'clock," Whitey Grey announced, his voice causing my heart to leap. "We gots to light a shuck."

"He'll come. . . ."

The albino muttered something and told Jasmine

to hush. "He ain't comin'. He's gutless. I've half a mind to go to that orphanage and slit his throat. Half a mind to slit you two's as well. Don't fancy leavin' that boy behind to spill his guts. And I tol' you this was an all or nothin' deal, so iffen I was to leave you behind . . . which would be my right, 'cause I said I would . . . you could blame that yeller friend of your'n, but I gots a generous disposition, so I'll take you two along with me. But by all rights, I should. . . ." He struggled for the word. "I should dis- . . . un- . . . I should just gets that gold and leave you chil'ren at that orphanage. Be five thousand more dollars for me to spend."

"He's coming. I know he's coming." I gave my friend the vote of confidence.

"We ain't waitin', one way or t'uther. Let's walk."

"But. . . ."

"I ramrod this outfit. You tots sure ain't givin' me no orders. Get a-movin'. That train won't wait. It's time."

"How can you tell?" Jasmine asked. "You can't see your watch."

"Ain't gots no watch to see nohow. Whitey Grey don't need no watch to tell the time. I know." I assume he tapped his chest, maybe his temple, for I heard a slight *thumping*. "I know in here. But we ain't waitin'. So come along, or I'll bury you in this mine."

For the next three miles, as we walked in the night, carrying only a canteen, war bag, and hopes, I kept wondering what had happened to Ian Spencer Henry. He had sounded as if he wanted to come more than any of us. Maybe his father had caught him trying to sneak out. Who knew? I looked over my shoulder several times, but saw only the glow of

light from town at first, and then only the faint outline of the desert. No friend.

No rattlesnakes, either, which was good.

The old stage road carried us straight to Lordsburg, and we heard a dog barking long before we
saw the flaring lights from the lantern at the depot.
Whitey Grey stopped in front of us and dropped into
a crouch. Jasmine and I stood, waiting, wondering.

"Don't likes the sound of that dog," he said at last
in a whisper. "Train comin' should be a freight, a
long one, so we'll cut 'cross here, hide in the brush
'bout twenty yards from the depot. Town's growed
some. You chil'ren stay quiet."

I'd been up to Lordsburg just the past week, helping Mr. Shankin haul down supplies from the railroad, and I didn't see how this town could have
grown. It had always drawn travelers, Apaches, soldiers, and ne'er-do-wells because of the natural
spring, filling their gourds, barrels, and canteens
while traveling to El Paso, Tucson, or points south of
the border. The Mormon Battalion marched through
here, Mr. Shankin had told me, back in 1846, and I
knew all about Butterfield's stagecoaches and the
Southern Pacific.

Yet the town, established by the railroad only a
year or two ago, remained mostly tent saloons and
uninviting *jacales*. Even the depot lacked the look of
anything permanent. The dog still barked, but he
sounded far away, at least nowhere in the vicinity of
the depot.

When we reached the rails, when it finally hit me
that Ian Spencer Henry wasn't coming, I felt betrayed. By Ian Spencer Henry, who had let me down.
By the white-skinned stranger who had refused to
wait, to give a boy a few extra minutes.

A whistle sounded in the night.

"Like I said," Whitey Grey spoke evenly, "that train don't wait. She'll take water here, but that's all, so we'll have to find a car, hope there ain't no railroad thugs or some surly boss with a nightstick. We'll ride to Stein's, get off there. Now, follow me, and keep your fly traps shut up tight."

The headlamp flickered in the east, and I tripped over the rail, pitching headfirst into the sand, then scrambled to my feet and raced into the rocks with Jasmine and the stranger.

Waiting.

Slowly the light grew larger, the metallic noises of the locomotive louder—heavy *creaks*, the grinding of gears and metal, *hissing* steam. Then the blinding light lit up the rocks. For the first time that night, I saw Jasmine's frightened face and the wild eyes of Whitey Grey as he hugged the earth while searching the train as it passed, and just like that, as the engine moved past us, the darkness returned, although fainter now, while the train slowed, slowed, and stopped.

Cries and shouts, muffled by the release of steam and the noise of the locomotive, sang out in the night. Whitey Grey's joints popped as he rose.

"Let's move, chil'ren," he said, and we followed, more from sound than sight, although by now, with the light from the engine's cab and caboose, as well as from the depot just down the tracks, it was easier to see, we could at least make out the freights toward the rear of the train.

"Here's one." Grunting, Whitey Grey slid the heavy door open, unleashing the scent of manure and straw. "You first, li'l' girlie." He scooped up Jasmine and tossed her through the opening.

Without a word, the albino whirled, grabbed me and hurled me inside, then with a grunt, he pulled himself into the livestock car. A horse grunted. Another stamped a nervous hoof on the floor, and, with a sudden lurch, the train pulled forward, slowly, creeping along slowly, past the depot, past the road to Shakespeare, heading into the desert again, moving slowly, methodically.

"Ol' Whitey Grey knows what he's doin', eh, chil'ren?" The strange man laughed, slapped his knees. A match flared. "Let's take a look-see," he said, and the flame roared larger. He had lighted a rolled newspaper. Where it came from, I hadn't a clue, but, after hours of lengthy dark, the light felt reassuring.

Two horses stood hobbled in the rear of the car, with sacks of something stacked two feet high in one corner, the floor covered with old hay. The place had a musky smell. " 'Bout an hour or so, we'll hit Stein's, be that much closer to my gold," Whitey Grey said. "Yes, sir, ol' Whitey Grey knows. . . ."

He sprang to his knees, still holding the burning paper, then he swore, passing the makeshift torch to Jasmine, who was nearer, and, gripping his left hand on the wall, he leaned out. The train lurched, and he let out a girlish shout, almost fell from the train, slowly picking up speed. He swore again.

At last, I heard it.

"Wait for me! Don't leave me! It's me, Ian Spencer Henry! Wait! Wait up!"

"Fool kid. He'll wake up half the town. Hand me that fire." He snatched the paper, waving it frantically outside. "Best hope nobody sees this but him. Here, boy! You see my li'l' torch. Run to us. Run! Hurry!"

More speed, and then the paper flamed up, and out, but I could see the outline of Whitey Grey leaning out of the opening, his right hand stretching into the darkness.

The rhythm of the *clicking* wheels picked up tempo. The freight rocked as the train's speed increased.

My heart pounded.

"Run, Ian Spencer Henry!" Jasmine yelled. "Run!"

"I can't see y'all no more!"

"Run! Run!" I shouted.

"Hurry, boy! Watch them rails. Get run over, it'll mangle you somethin' fierce!"

"RUN!"

Clickety. Clickety. Clickety.

Faster. Faster. Faster.

Whitey Grey groaned, leaned forward. "Just one more. . . ."

And . . . he was gone.

A crash sounded, faint above the metallic noises of the train, followed by a curse, then Ian Spencer Henry's scream.

"Oh, no!" Jasmine yelled.

The freight rocked violently now, the wind blowing into the open car. In the darkness, cold wind numbed my face as I looked outside, but saw nothing.

"JACK! JASMINE!"

It was Ian Spencer Henry's voice.

"Shut up, kid!" Whitey Grey yelled back. We could just hear them over the train. The whistle blared again.

Both still lived. I mouthed a quick prayer.

"What'll we do, Jack?" Jasmine asked me, her voice so close, I was startled and almost fell off the rolling train.

The question took me by surprise. *What now? Indeed!*

The train lurched, wobbled, sped.

"JUMP! GET OFF THAT TRAIN!" Whitey Grey screamed, ignoring his own admonishments for quiet, but his voice sounded fainter, growing farther and farther away.

While the train rolled faster, I felt Jasmine's hand grab mine.

"Jack?" she asked.

I peered into the darkness, wind whooshing through my hair.

"JUMP!" the albino screamed. Ian Spencer Henry echoed his voice in a distant shout.

Jump.

I looked at Jasmine Allison, saw only a faint outline. I squeezed her hand, felt her return the action, and without a word, as the whistle blared somewhere ahead of us, we leaped into the nothingness.

Chapter Seven

Somewhere, during our brief flight, Jasmine and I had let go of one another. Probably a good thing, for I surmise we could have broken our arms, and it's a miracle neither of us cracked our necks, or any bones, in the mêlée that followed. I landed on my feet. At least, I think I did, immediately ricocheting off the sand and brush, spinning head over heels in the air, to crash even harder on my back, tumbling here and there, a roaring in my ears—perhaps that sound came from the train, now speeding along at close to fifteen miles an hour—as I bounded, rolled, and ached my way near the rails. I seem to recall seeing the light from inside the caboose as it rolled on past. Maybe, though, I just saw stars.

In any event, I slid to a rest on my face, head pounding, ears ringing, nose and lips leaking blood and sand, both ankles throbbing. I pushed myself up on my arms, gasping for air, shaking my head, spitting out sand, then fell face down again.

"No time for that, boy. We gots to move out *muy pronto* on the ankle express." The voice, Whitey Grey's, sounded so far away, but the toe of his shabby boot felt all too near when it poked my aching ribs.

"Ups. Run, boy. All of you! Railroad curs is comin'!"

Barks and shouts penetrated my ringing ears. Opening my eyes, I made out a torch, then another, heard an Irish voice curse the Apaches, which startled me before I understood that the men from the Lordsburg depot thought *we* were the Apaches.

"Come, on," a gentler voice whispered, and Ian Spencer Henry helped me to my feet. Weaving unsteadily, I took a few tentative steps before remembering something.

"Jasmine?"

"I'm all right," she said a few rods up the tracks. "Think I am. . . ."

The albino swore another oath, then his footsteps sounded as he ran westward into the night.

Savage barks. More shouts. The torches kept creeping closer. Swallowing blood and sand, I suggested that we follow the albino. "Can you run?" I called out to Jasmine.

Her footsteps answered me.

Dawn found us by the *playas* southwest of Lordsburg, where I saw, in addition to felt, just how hard a tumble I had taken. Dried blood, peppered with sand, caked the left side of my face, and the shape of my nose told me it had been broken. The pinky finger on my left hand seemed crooked, and I couldn't bend it, the palm badly skinned, while my right shirt sleeve was torn into strips, arm and hand criss-crossed with scratches. My ankles still hurt, but if I had walked five or more miles, nothing had been busted.

Cool, alkaline water burned my hands as I dipped them into the water, shattering my reflection, and began to wash my face and slake my thirst.

"Fall rains, summer monsoons been good," Whitey Grey said. "Water ain't always so plentiful, but don't drink too much of it."

He didn't have to warn me. The salty water burned more than relieved, but at least it reduced my swollen tongue's size.

"Tolerable." Ian Spencer Henry, acting like some savvy frontiersman in a Beadle and Adams half-dime tale, spit out a mouthful. "I've had worse."

With a grunt, Whitey Grey opened a pewter flask, which contained something even stronger than the *playas* offering of water.

"We have to cross . . . *that?*" Jasmine's face paled.

She hadn't been banged up as much as I had. Oh, her sleeves were ripped, and bruises were beginning to form on her forehead and hands, and she walked gingerly, favoring her left leg. I followed her gaze, staring across the flat, hard land beyond the small pool of water. We stared off into *Valle de las Playas*, an infinity of nothing, the sand already reflecting the rising sun's heat. Even in early October, crossing the old lake bed could be like stepping into a furnace. The water I had just drank no longer tasted so bad, but I remembered Whitey Grey's warning, and knew he was right. Too much would make me sick.

When my father still dreamed and acted like a father, when we had first arrived in Shakespeare, he had told my mother, sisters, and me all about the great dead lakes between Shakespeare and Arizona Territory. Once, he had said, more than 12,000 years ago, these lakes had been as vast and full and magnificent as the Great Lakes of the north, filling much of the basin. Yet the climate had changed, warming and warming until southern New Mexico became an arid wasteland. Streams and lakes dried, leaving nothing but flat beds hard as nails, uncompromising, unforgiving. Water returned only during spring snow melt or from the violent thunderstorms, usually in late summer, and even then the liquid only lasted a brief while before disappearing into the desert.

Whitey Grey had been right. We were lucky to find water here.

He had led us—no, that's not right. He had taken off, to save himself, and we had followed, to save ourselves. I thought back to that night. For some reason, the dog, or dogs, had kept their distance, as did our human pursuers. Whitey turned north from the rails, and Jasmine, Ian Spencer Henry, and I stumbled along after him, darting through cactus and brush, in and out of arroyos, eventually turning back south and west. We had stopped only once, and now our pursuers had given up their search and retired back to the comforts of Lordsburg. With the skies turning gray in the east, we had slaked our thirst slightly from Ian Spencer Henry's canteen.

Jasmine had left her canteen in the freight car. Mine lay somewhere along the tracks of the Southern Pacific, along with my war bag of clean clothes, jerky, and sardines.

"Bet you're glad I come along," my friend had said. "Else, you'd be a mite parched."

He reminded us of our luck now, sitting on the edge of the *playa*, holding up his canteen for Jasmine to see. "Don't worry, girlie," he said, imitating the white-skinned treasure hunter, "I got a canteen, and I'll share."

This led to a snort from Whitey Grey. "Hey, what happened to your gear? Your water? Y'all had it back in town. I knowed 'cause I heard it sloshin' all night when we was walkin' up from Shakespeare."

When we informed him of our losses, he cursed and let the flask disappear into his pocket. "Well, by my boots and socks, that just 'bout tears it. Water's life in this country, chil'ren." His head shook savagely and he let out a mirthless laugh. "I can hear Scott McKenzie up in Detroit, sayin' what a fool I am, and I've half a mind to agree with him. Ain't nobody would blame me none if I let you fools fend for yourselves out here, just struck out on my own. Nobody would blame me. They'd say ol' Whitey Grey finally showed good sense."

"I got mine!" Ian Spencer Henry proudly held up his canvas bag and canteen.

Yeah, I thought, *but what's in that bag? Dime novels and nonsense?*

Unimpressed, Whitey Grey spat. "What do I need you chil'ren for anyway?"

That's a question I had always wondered. He stood, his knees popping, and slapped dust off his hat. He had taken quite a violent spill when he had slipped—or Ian Spencer Henry had pulled him—off the train, and his cuts and bruises looked much more fiendish against his deathly pale skin.

"One canteen. Well, you ain't havin' none of mine. That's for certain sure. Nary a drop. You can fetch some for yourself when we reach Stein's Peak or Doubtful Cañon. If we reach it . . . if you reach it . . . alive."

Ian Spencer Henry hesitated, then topped off his canteen with the alkaline water of the lake.

"We ain't crossin' that country," the albino said, his voice softer now, his wrath lessened. "Not all of it, nohow. We'll cut south now, head back to the S.P. Maybe I'll get lucky, for once."

And, for once, luck shined on Whitey Grey. We had made it back to the Southern Pacific, began pushing our weary bodies westward along the tracks, bene-fiting from a cloudy day. Maybe we had walked an-other mile or two when the albino stopped, stared, rubbed his eyes, then gripped the butt of his re-volver.

The sight took me by surprise, too, when I peered around Whitey Grey's back and down the tracks lined with telegraph poles on one side, and nothing on the other. At first, I took it to be a mirage, some apparition, as my mouth hung open. Behind me, I felt Jasmine's arm on my shoulder, then heard Ian Spencer Henry's question.

"Should we hide?"

Two of the oddest conveyances I had ever seen came barreling down the tracks, straight for us. Un-derstand, I had grown up around the railroads but had never spied anything like those two three-wheeled vehicles headed our way, one driven by a man in striped denim britches and an Irish woolen cap, the second by a red-bearded man wearing a dun-colored cap.

Not exactly bicycles. Certainly not the boxy hand-cars with pump handles often used by railroad construction crews. Oddly silent. The driver sat be-tween the two-wheeled bicycle-like machine—it didn't look comfortable—with an axle extending from just behind the front flanged wheel and across the tracks, where the third, much smaller, wheel, also flanged, rolled along the far rail, I presumed for balance. The only noise came from the drivers, grunting from the push-pull motions it took to run the fantastic devices.

The first man saw us and yelped at his trailing comrade, who stood up a bit on the pedals, then pulled a lever-action rifle from behind his seat. Their vehicles slowed, but the first man, still staring at us, said something else, and the red-bearded man nodded. On they came, slowing as they neared.

"Hide?" Finally Whitey Grey answered Ian Spencer Henry's question with a sarcastic laugh. "From salvation?" He stepped forward, releasing his grip on his revolver, removed his battered hat, and waved it toward the men.

"Hallooooo!" he called out. "You're a sight for God-fearin' eyes."

"I . . . how . . . what on earth?" The red-bearded man removed his cap and scratched his bald head. The man in the striped britches and woolen cap found himself equally at a loss for words.

They stepped off the vehicles as if dismounting a horse, the red-bearded man keeping his rifle ready, but never pointing it toward us. Whitey Grey laughed and slapped my back so hard, I almost fell to my knees. Next, he offered his right hand to both men, who reluctantly took it, if only briefly.

"Never seen nothin' like 'em things afore," Whitey Grey said.

"New," the first man said. "From the George S. Sheffield and Company of Three Rivers, Michigan. They call it a velocipede car."

The brace connecting the third wheel, less than a foot in diameter, held the velocipede, with its 24-inch wheels, upright. Ball bearings, a driving chain and gears, handlebars, cranks, and pedals. Progress amazed me. The first man patted his ride. The second looked more interested in keeping the rifle handy, ready.

" 'Tain't no mule or horse," Whitey Grey said, still staring at the velocipedes. "Michigan, eh? I was up in Michigan a spell. Detroit. Too cold for my likin'."

"Mister," the red-bearded man said, his voice on the surly side, "what are you-all doing out here?"

"Caught these here runaways," the white-skinned man lied. "Run off from the orphanage in Shakespeare. I'm supposed to deliver 'em to this nun or her hired boy at Stein's Peak."

"Orphanage?" the striped-britches man said in astonishment. "Shakespeare?"

The man with the rifle said: "Stein's?"

"Yeah," Whitey Grey said, and his ability at telling lies, his embellishments, and fast-thinking astonished me. "I wasn't sure when or where I'd catch up with these here chil'ren. I tell you, boys, they was a-footin' it. Almost made it to Silver City afore I slicked 'em. That's why I'm supposed to meet that sister at the station in Stein's. Lost my horse 'bout ten miles north of here. I'd be grateful if you could let us borrow 'em centipede cars and deliver 'em. That nun, I mean she's worried sick. Frail thing. Must be nigh eighty year old."

"Shakespeare?" the first man repeated.

The second man's finger slipped inside the Winchester's trigger guard.

"They's a reward," Whitey Grey said. "Hunnert dollars. I be of a mind to split it with you, say give you each twenty-five." He slapped his hand on his dusty britches. "Or even just rent 'em things . . . I'll need both of 'em with these chil'ren . . . for fifty and give you a little rye whiskey for the walk home. Either way you fancy it."

The second man put his thumb on the rifle's hammer.

The first man said: "Mister, there ain't no orphanage in Shakespeare."

"Not a real one," Jasmine fired off. "Not officially. It's part of the church." She kept adding to her lies, and I found her pretty skilled at it, too. Ian Spencer Henry's mouth fell open in wonderment. I watched the two strangers, their eyes full of suspicion.

"They just started in within the last month," Jasmine said. "To help all the kids who lost their parents. Big cave-in, you know. And a diphtheria epidemic. You-all haven't heard?"

Even Whitey Grey looked puzzled.

"I don't want to go back," Jasmine added. "They beat me. See." She showed her bruises and the cuts on her hands.

The first man asked Jasmine: "What church?"

"Methodist." She answered too fast, without thinking, and I cringed. My friend's newfound ability at lying had limits. *A nun at an orphanage run by Methodists?* I thought angrily. *Come on, Jasmine. Think!*

"Little sister," said the first man, "there ain't no Methodist church in Shakespeare."

"It just started," Jasmine tried.

"Ain't no Presbyterian church. No Catholic. No Israelite temple."

"No God in Shakespeare, neither," the second man was saying, and in a quick motion his rifle bore now trained on Whitey Grey's gut.

The silence that followed didn't last long, for suddenly Whitey Grey let out a loud howl, and ran his rough fingers through Jasmine's hair. "That was a good try, li'l' girlie." He patted her head, slapped his hat on his head, and nodded at the two railroaders. The Winchester, however, never moved.

"Mister," the first man said, "you best tell us the truth. What in the Sam Hill are you and these kids doing out here? No more lies. Max and me, we're in a hurry to get to Lordsburg alive."

"Thought you might be Apaches," said the man called Max. "You look like you run into some."

"Apaches?" Whitey Grey chuckled again, but he wet his lips and looked concerned more than irritated. "What you talkin' 'bout?"

"Great Scot, man," said the first man. "You ain't heard?"

"Heard what?"

"Heard about the ruction at San Carlos," the first man answered. "Big fight at Cibecue Creek. Scouts turned on the Army, who was trying to arrest that dreamer holy man. Wiped out Carr's entire command is what we've heard. Then a slew of them jumped the reservation. Max and me figger they aim to steal and murder their way to the border, join up with ol' Nana in Sonora. So does the Army and the S.P. Be a bloodbath for sure."

Before the man finished, Whitey Grey, his face even paler, sank to his knees, and he just squatted there, shaking his head, struck dumb, his mouth open, eyes distant.

"We come to repair the wire between here and Stein's," the man with the rifle called Max added. "Apaches. Now we aim to get back to Lordsburg."

Said the first man: "I sure feel sorry for that woman and her guide."

"Yeah," the man called Max addressed the first man, "but Mister Sparks warned her that Doubtful Cañon's no place to be."

Mention of that place brought the albino back to us.

"What woman? What about Doubtful Cañon?"

Max answered. "Some gal from Texas showed up at Lordsburg, hired Willie Spoon to take her to the cañon. Says her old man got killed by Apaches there twenty years ago, and she wants to find the place and put a marker on her pa's grave. Blame foolishness from a fool petticoat."

"And her name?" Whitey asked. "Or her pa's name?"

"Giddings," the first man replied. "I know that because I was in Giddings, Texas, when they hung Bloody Bill Longley two, three years back."

Now the albino fell onto his backside, shaking his head. "What about ol' Whitey Grey, Lord?" he said, looking at the sky. "Can't nothin' go right for this tired soul? Twenty years. Twenty years I spend waitin', come down from Detroit at long last, wait for Victorio to get kilt, wait for Nana to finish his bloody business, wait till there's some sort of peace in this country. And once I get here, what do you give me, Lord? Ill-mannered chil'ren, the baddest luck I ever got dealt, then you set the Apaches on the prod and send that hard-rock Giddings's daughter after my gold! 'Tain't fair, Lord. It just ain't fair!"

Chapter Eight

"What in blazes are you talking about?" the first man asked.

Said the second, a little more urgently: "What gold?"

"Forget him, Max." The first man turned to mount the lead velocipede car. "He ain't got no gold. He's crazy as a loon. Let's get out of this country while we're still alive. I ain't waiting for any Apache buck to come back and cut that wire again. Next time, it might be old Nana himself, and I got a belly full of him this summer."

Shaking his head with a sigh, the man named Max lowered his Winchester and followed the first man, but the moment he had slid the rifle into a scabbard behind the second velocipede's seat, Whitey Grey revived and rose.

"Wait!" the albino commanded.

The man called Max turned, the rifle back in his arms.

"We're getting out of this country," the first man said. "You made it this far. You want to go back to Lordsburg, it's only seven, eight miles or so. Stein's? Well, that's about the same. Suit yourself."

"What about me?" Whitey Grey said. "There's twenty-five dollars in it. For both you fellers."

"I don't think you got twenty-five dollars," the first man said.

"There's gold," Whitey Grey said.

"Reckon Morgan is right. Can't spend gold if I'm dead." the red-bearded man called Max said. "And I don't think you have any gold, neither. Like Morgan says, you're loco. Some desert hermit with three rawhide kids. Now shuck that pistol of yours. I don't fancy getting shot in the back, neither."

Ignoring the command, Whitey Grey motioned toward Jasmine, Ian Spencer Henry, and me. "You'd leave me. That I understand," the white-skinned man said as he slowly approached the railroad conveyances. "But these here are chil'ren, not a one of 'em o'er ten years old." Well, he had decreased our years by two, but the point he made put the railroaders in a moral dilemma. "Leave me, that's all right, but you can't leave these boys and li'l' girlie behind. For if the Cherry Cows kill 'em, their blood'll be on your hands."

Now standing face-to-face with red-bearded Max, the albino clasped his hands. "All I'm askin'," he pleaded, "is for you to spare the chil'ren. Get 'em back to Lordsburg, send word to their kin in Hachita."

Hachita? Ian Spencer Henry and I shot each other a glance. Another mining camp, digging out silver, lead, copper, and even some turquoise, Hachita had sprung to life around 1875 and lay, from what I'd heard, more than twenty miles south of the Southern Pacific station at Separ, a long, dusty way from Shakespeare. Closer to Mexico than anywhere else.

Yet the railroaders studied Whitey Grey, and, hesitating, Max looked toward the children.

That's all Whitey Grey needed.

Never had the albino struck me as a quick man, and, despite all his threats and curses, I never thought of him as violent, but his right hand shot down for his ivory-handled Colt, while the left gripped the Winchester's barrel and jerked savagely. Before Max knew what had happened, Whitey Grey had split his ear with the long barrel of the revolver, then stepped back, pulling the Winchester from Max's grasp seconds before the railroader crumpled beside the velocipede car in a heap.

He took another step back, lifting the Colt at the first man named Morgan, whose arms shot skyward as he leaped off the driver's seat.

"Don't shoot!" the first man screamed.

Whitey Grey shot him anyway.

Bedlam followed. Ears ringing from the gunshot and the screams of Ian Spencer Henry, not Jasmine. Then he started running off into the desert in the general direction of Preacher Mountain. I just stood there, dazed, watching incredulously as Whitey Grey, his face animated and awful, walked around the metal vehicle toward the man named Morgan, who lay sprawled on the tracks. Ominously Whitey Grey thumbed back the Colt's hammer and aimed at the man's head.

"Murder!" the man shouted weakly, extending his right hand in a futile defensive move. "Murder! Murder!"

"You're not killing him!" Jasmine yelled, and before I, or the albino, understood what was happening, she had flung herself across the wounded man's body.

"Get up!" Whitey Grey commanded. "Up, li'l' girlie, or I'll shoot you both."

The man named Max groaned, causing the albino to spin and make sure the man he had buffaloed posed no threat. An instant later, he spotted me, and, in a flash, I found myself staring down the bore of his large-caliber Colt.

"Put that rock down, boy, or your brains'll be splattered all over this country, you cussed li'l' sneak."

"Jack!" Jasmine cried.

Only then did I notice the rock in my right hand, held above my head. I must have been creeping toward the albino, bound to protect Jasmine, although I didn't remember picking up the stone, which now fell from my sore fingers.

The man named Max groaned.

Whitey Grey shook his head, turned back toward the man he had shot, when suddenly, from out of nowhere, charged Ian Spencer Henry, wailing like a pirate, leaping onto the albino's back. The pistol roared. So did I.

Like a bull I coursed, lowering my shoulder and crashing into Whitey Grey's knees, wrapping my arms around his legs, knocking him to the ground while Ian Spencer Henry flailed about with his tiny fists. The albino screamed, cursed, hit. Jasmine, joining the affair, kicked, scratched, and bit. We rolled over rails and ties, gravel and sand, hitting the metal railroad vehicles and each other.

"*Ow!*" Ian Spencer Henry yelled. "That's me!"

"Sorry."

Dust stung my eyes. My bent pinky finger throbbed in pain. My busted, bruised, banged nose began spilling blood once more. Someone kicked me in the chest. Ian Spencer Henry yelled something ridiculous from one of his five-penny dreadfuls. Jasmine yanked on the albino's ragged curls.

The man named Max groaned.

The other railroader, the man named Morgan with a bullet in his left shoulder, crawled toward the Colt Whitey Grey had dropped.

A knee came up, and I rode with it, then a ragged boot rocketed me into the air. When I landed, the breath *whooshed* out of my lungs, and I lay there, stunned, spread-eagled, shaking my head a few moments later, trying to regain my faculties.

"That tears it!"

Slowly I sat up, watching Ian Spencer Henry go spinning down the tracks like a top, tottering, before tripping and toppling over the second velocipede car's axle-rod. Jasmine sat a few feet away, legs stretched out before her, rubbing her temples slowly. Only Whitey Grey stood, and he turned, kicked the first man in the face, and sent him rolling across the rails, whining and bleeding. The albino reached down and picked up his Colt, blowing dust and sand from the cylinder before shoving it in his pants and grabbing the Winchester.

"Mutinous li'l' curs," Whitey Grey said, his eyes falling on me first, then a dizzy Ian Spencer Henry, finally on poor Jasmine Allison. "I ramrod this outfit. Try that again and you'll wish the Apaches had catched you alive."

He sucked on his left forefinger, spit, and kicked the groaning man named Max back into unconsciousness. After fishing out his flask and having a couple of swallows, he walked back to the man he had shot.

"How bad you hurt?" he asked, his voice shockingly polite, suddenly calm.

"I don't know," the railroader whined.

"Well, serves you right. Let me look at that."

Slowly I pulled myself to my feet and staggered toward the voices.

"You'll live. Didn't hit no bone. Stick that handkerchief in that hole. Stop the bleedin'."

The albino gave me only a glance, then pointed the Winchester's barrel at the railroader's throat.

"Please. . . ." The man began sobbing.

"Shut up. And buck up. You railroad men gots no spine. Now I aim to ask you a few questions, and you better answer me. Gots a fiercesome temper. You seen that already, but I've cooled off a mite now. But if I gets riled again, I might just accidental-like pull on this." His finger patted the trigger while his thumb eared back the hammer. "That would be plumb awful."

Ian Spencer Henry and Jasmine gathered around. We said nothing, fearing we might somehow fuel the albino's rage.

"What's this 'bout the Apaches?"

"They killed Colonel Carr and his entire command. Max read about it in a New York Times he'd found in one of the smoking cars. Late August. His scouts turned on him when they went up to arrest this holy man at San Carlos."

Whitey Grey's dead eyes blinked, trying to fathom the news.

"Just some of 'em Apache bucks the Army hired to scout?" he asked hopefully. "That what you mean?"

The railroader shook his head meekly. "It's a lot more than just a few renegade scouts. Mister Sparks, he's my boss, he got the wire the other day."

"Uhn-huh."

"Late sometime on the night of September Thirtieth . . . that's, what, three, four days back, about half the Chiricahuas at San Carlos pulled out, run off toward Mexico. Scared after what happened at Cibecue, what might happen to them. Army fears that they'll join up with Nana down in Sonora, and come back across the border. One of those Apaches that left is named Geronimo, and he's a mean one. Then the wire went dead. Yesterday, Mister Sparks sent Max and me out on the Sheffield cars to check the line."

"And?"

"Found it. Fixed it. Took some time. They'd spliced it with a rubber band, made it hard for Max and me to spot. That's an old Apache trick. Unshod pony and moccasin tracks all around, too. I remember Victorio. . . ."

Whitey Grey cut him off with an oath, then, sighing heavily, he closed his eyes and lowered the Winchester's barrel.

The railroader sat up a little, grimacing, one hand pressed against the bloody rag in his shoulder. "I . . . I . . . could use . . . some water." He addressed Jasmine, who looked at me for an answer.

Yet before I could suggest that Ian Spencer Henry share his canteen, Whitey Grey's eyes opened and he jammed the rifle barrel underneath the railroader's Adam's apple.

Nearby, the man named Max groaned.

"And what's this 'bout the Giddings gal?" Whitey Grey asked.

"Water?" the man called Morgan begged.

"After you answer me."

He coughed, grunted. His head bobbed. "She got off the train at Lordsburg on Friday . . . no, reckon it was Thursday, right before the Apaches lit a shuck. Comely woman, barely in her twenties. Said her pa was killed by Apaches in April of 'Sixty-One at Doubtful Cañon. She never knew him, but wanted to see that he got a good Christian grave. Mister Sparks, he warned her that Doubtful Cañon's no place for a woman."

The railroader coughed and winced, and Whitey Grey relented, offering him the flask of whiskey. That led to a few more savage coughs after the man swallowed.

"You were sayin'?" the albino prodded with lessening patience.

"That brew's wickeder than Taos Lightning," the railroader said, but he took another swallow from the flask just the same.

Whitey Grey tapped the trigger with his finger.

"All right, all right," the man named Morgan said. "Mister Sparks said she shouldn't go, that just a few months ago old Nana was killing and maiming, and, even when he wasn't, that cañon is always full of snakes, those with two legs and those that just crawl."

"But she went?"

"Yeah. Lady's got grit. Willie Spoon crawled out of Pegleg Murphey's tent saloon, said he'd take Miss Giddings to her pa's grave for ten dollars."

"How'd he know where that grave is?" Whitey Grey asked. "Been twenty years, and there's been plenty of buryin' done at Doubtful Cañon afore and since."

"Yeah, but Willie, he's a fixture in the territory like wind and dust. Says he was freighting then, and come across the ruins of Stein's Peak station right after the fight. Remembered the stagecoach, everything, even recalled the girl's daddy being full of arrows. And . . . that the animals that had gotten to him after the Apaches had done their dirty work."

"She believed him?"

"Yes, sir."

"This Spoon gent, he mention any survivor from that fracas?"

"Said they found some Overland gunman at what was left of Stein's. Took him on to Tucson. That's all. Anyhow, Spoon's story sounded gospel to Miss Giddings. So, come first light, they left."

The albino pondered this. "Should be back by now," he said.

"If the Apaches or bandits haven't killed them," the railroader said.

"Or. . . ." Whitey Grey lowered the rifle, pushed back his hat brim, and slowly stood. "Or iffen they're lookin' for somethin' other than a grave."

The man cleared his throat. "I sure could use some water," he said, his voice hoarse.

"Yeah." Whitey Grey slammed the rifle barrel against the railroader's head. He fell hard onto the tracks, and the albino brought the stock of the rifle to his shoulder and aimed at the unconscious man's head.

"You're a mean, mean man!" Jasmine yelled. "And if you kill him, I'll . . . I'll. . . ."

"Yeah," Ian Spencer Henry said.

The white-skinned man glared at my friends.

"We said we'd go with you." I had found my voice. "But we won't be part of any murder. If you kill these men, you'll have to kill us."

"Jack!" Ian Spencer Henry glared at me.

I don't know why I said that. I'd never been one to gamble, and I really had no idea why the albino wanted us along on this adventure, an adventure rapidly becoming a nightmare, but he did seem to value us.

"I tol' you chil'ren I ramrod this outfit," the wild man said. "Tol' you that a hunnert times."

"Yes," I answered, "but we're not murderers. Not for five thousand dollars. Not for thirty thousand."

He swung the rifle toward me, grinning wickedly. "Last chance, Jack Dunivan," he said.

I closed my eyes. "No, sir." My voice came out as a choked whisper.

Next, I heard the albino's crazy laugh, and, when I forced my eyelids up, the Winchester rested on his shoulder, the hammer lowered, and he motioned toward the railroader on the tracks. "Drag his carcass off the tracks. Don't want him gettin' runned over by no S.P. train, chil'ren. They can walk back to Lordsburg when they come to."

Jasmine and Ian Spencer Henry ran to their chore before the albino could change his mind. I couldn't move. To be honest, shaking so badly, I felt amazed that I could still stand.

"And when you're finished with him, haul this other gent away from the rails." Whitey Grey slid the rifle into the scabbard, thought of something, and walked back to the red-bearded man, going through his clothes, coming away with a half-used plug of tobacco, a piece of jerky, a few dollars and change in coin, and an open-faced, silver watch. Next, as Ian Spencer Henry and Jasmine Allison dragged Max a safe distance from the rails, Whitey Grey robbed Morgan.

"Here." He flung the Irish woolen cap toward me. "You'll need this."

I hadn't realized that I had lost my straw hat during my leap off the train.

"Now, my li'l' pardners," Whitey Grey said, "all aboard."

"I don't want to go with you no more," Jasmine said. "I don't like you."

"You been conscripted," the albino said. "And the penalty for desertion is a firin' squad, or maybe just a bullet in the head. Y'all take stock in that. I'm lettin' these fellers live, but if you cross me again, I won't be so charitable."

"They'll need water." I nodded at the unconscious railroaders. "It's a long walk to Lordsburg."

"'Tain't that far," he said. "They can find the *playas* iffen they gets thirsty. Now stop your jawin', boy." He removed his hat, scratched his head, and muttered: "You chil'ren got any notion as to how you make these centipede cars go?"

Chapter Nine

Maneuvering the George S. Sheffield & Company velocipede cars required muscle, for each weighed around 140 pounds. Ian Spencer Henry and I inspected the conveyances, urged by Whitey Grey to hurry before the railroaders began to stir.

"They's goin' the wrong way, chil'ren," the albino told us.

During our examination, Jasmine Allison walked over and pointed to the brace rod that connected the third wheel. After that discovery, we figured everything out, and Whitey Grey went to work, unhooking the rod, which swung to the frame, then grunting as he lifted the vehicle and turned it around. Now we worked together, bringing the rod back, hooking it in place, and securing the flanged wheel on the far rail. The flanged front wheel and the guide wheel would keep the car in place, while the rear wheel, much wider than the rails, looked safe enough. I didn't think it would slip off the track.

"There." I dusted my hands.

When the velocipede car didn't tumble over, we redirected the other machine until both pointed westward down the line.

"You sit here." Suddenly taking charge, I instructed

Whitey Grey. "You steer the front wheel with this."
I patted the handlebars. "Around curves and such."

His head bobbed slightly, but he approached the
metal vehicle with trepidation, wetting his lips,
slowly reaching out, cooing as if he were trying to
mount a skittish bronco.

'Tain't no horse, he had said earlier, and I would
have smiled if not for the fact that the albino now
frightened me, even more than he had when he had
chased us from the Lady Macbeth Mine. "There's
only two seats, one on each velocipede," I said after
Whitey Grey mounted the Sheffield car without getting bucked off. "I'll take the other car. We'll have to
leave Jasmine and Ian Spencer Henry behind." I
swallowed down fear, wondering if he would accept
my proposal, hoping he wouldn't just kill my friends
in a bit of rage.

"No," he said.

"But. . . ."

"No buts. You, Jack Dunivan, you ride that centipede car in the front, and don't get no fancy notions.
Boy"—he nodded at Ian Spencer Henry—"you sit
right behind him. Hold him tight, 'cause if you's to
fall off, you might get trampled by my centipede
car." No longer did he look nervous. His resolve had
returned. "Li'l' girlie, you hop on right behind ol'
Whitey Grey and get a good hold around my paunch.
And don't you boys spur that thing into no gallop,
'cause if I gets to thinkin' you's tryin' to leave me
behind, well, that contraption ain't likely to outrun
no Forty-Four-Forty bullet. Y'all savvy?"

Reluctantly I climbed onto the first car, gripped
the bar, and waited for Ian Spencer Henry to take
his place behind me on the uncomfortable metal
bench. "How come you get to drive?" he said in a

hoarse whisper before letting out a sigh of disappointment.

The men named Max and Morgan moaned.

"Light a shuck, boys!" the albino yelled. "We's burnin' daylight!"

And so we rode.

Starting off proved a struggle, but once the bicycles—would that be, *tricycles?*—on rails built up speed, once we learned to let the cars do most of the work, the vehicles moved surprisingly smooth and fast, gliding down the tracks, pushed by a slight tailwind.

"Don't make much noise, do they, Jack?" Ian Spencer Henry said after we had traveled a mile.

"Probably for safety," I suggested. "Need to hear any train coming."

The desert passed before us, and I found a rhythm in the motion of the Sheffield car, enjoying the wind in my face, the speed, almost forgetting about Whitey Grey behind me with the Winchester rifle until he called out for us to halt.

Only then did I notice the rugged mountain stretching out before us, shadowing a rickety shed and weather-beaten water tower. After stopping the Sheffield velocipede, I looked behind me as Ian Spencer Henry stepped off and stretched his legs and rubbed his buttocks.

"Stein's Peak," Whitey Grey said. "Let's get these contraptions off the tracks. Don't want 'em to get mangled by no passin' train. We'll hide 'em in the brush. Might come in handy when we gets my gold. They don't take no food and water like a hoss or mule, but they ain't so comfortable on my ol' knees and hindquarters." Pointing the Winchester barrel at the tool box behind my seat, he added: "And let's open that and see if 'em railroaders packed somethin' useful. Then we'll bust in that shed, steal us some picks and shovels. Oh, and one other thing. . . ."

Savagely he grabbed Jasmine's arm and shoved her toward us, brought the rifle to his shoulder, and eared back the hammer. "You chil'ren been playin' ol' Whitey Grey for a fool, and I ain't no fool. You think I done forgotten 'bout what happened with 'em railroaders? I ain't. My brain don't forgets a thing. There ain't no orphanage in Shakespeare. You chil'ren lied to me. Now, give me the truth, or I might get riled."

My friends stared at me, again electing me spokesman, and slowly I let the truth out, skimming over some of the personal tragedies involved, just trying to make the albino understand that our parents— my drunkard father, Ian Spencer Henry's preoccupied dad, and Jasmine's fallen mother—most likely would jump for joy at our departure, if they ever noticed our absence.

It didn't set well with Whitey Grey.

"They'll come lookin'," he said with a snarl. "I should put you asunder now, be shun of you and your troubles. Law might charge me with kidnappin', child stealin', and I don't fancy spendin' no time in the territorial pen up in Santa Fé. No, sir. Never been charged with child stealin' afore."

Ian Spencer Henry cried out his argument: "By the time my pa finds out the truth, we'll be back in Shakespeare with our money and you'll be long gone."

"We wrote a note," Jasmine offered. "Jack left a note for them to find in the mine. It says we've run off to El Paso. No one will think to look out here."

The white-skinned man didn't hear them. His hollow eyes stared off toward the rugged peak. " 'Course, iffen you three was to turn up dead hereabouts, laws might put the blame on 'em renegade Apache bucks. That's a notion to consider."

He stared back at me, and my throat went dry, my eyes darting from the Winchester on his shoulder to the Colt stuck in his waistband. Would he have killed us? I'm not sure, for Whitey Grey kept proving to be a difficult man to read, but he seemed to be leaning toward that option when a whistle blasted all four of us out of our wits.

The crazed adult recovered first, moving back and forth, hollering at us to take cover behind the rocks beyond the water tower. "It's the eastbound!" he yelled. "Get out of sight!"

When Ian Spencer Henry didn't move fast enough, Whitey Grey picked him up and effortlessly tossed him over the outcropping, then herded Jasmine in the general direction, and at last turned toward me. I needed no more encouragement, and certainly preferred the route Jasmine had taken over that of Ian Spencer Henry's. The hard, metallic *clicks* and groans grew closer as the Southern Pacific crept over the barren pass, coughing and puffing, slowing, *squeaking, hissing* . . . yet never stopping.

I peered around the natural rock wall after making sure Ian Spencer Henry had not broken his neck. "That smarts," was all he said, as he sat up, rubbing his shoulder.

"You're a wicked old man!" Jasmine told our jailer.

"Hush," he said, Winchester in his arms, his dead eyes keen. "Don't you chil'ren get no notions 'bout runnin', neither."

The train rumbled on now, picking up speed, moving with an urgency to get through this rough, abysmal country. In a moment, all we could see were the clouds, then tendrils of black smoke, and soon even those had vanished in the desert.

"It didn't even stop for water!" Jasmine exclaimed.

"Ain't no water here." The albino lowered the hammer on the rifle and stood, his knees *creaking*. "Nearest water's six, seven miles up the road, at the old station. Fool railroaders tried diggin', but they might as well go all the way to China afore they'd ever find nothin' wet. No, sir, chil'ren, the onliest thing this patch of ground's good for is holdin' the two ends of the earth together."

I found no fault in his assessment. The country lacked color, looked crude, raw, ugly. In years to come, it would support a small town—water being hauled down and sold for $1 a barrel—after gold, silver, lead, and copper were discovered in the Peloncillo Mountains north of here, taking first the name Doubtful Cañon and later Steins, but even those ventures would prove relatively short-lived. In the autumn of 1881, the place looked as far removed from civilization as anything I had ever witnessed. Even the rawhide water tower—indeed, now I could tell it had never been finished—and the small shed seemed out of place. No wonder that train had hurried through this place. I felt the urge to run myself.

"'Tain't pretty," Whitey Grey said as he walked around the rocks and toward the shed, guarded by only cactus. He had forgotten about his thoughts of murdering us, and we weren't about to remind him.

The lock had already been broken, most of the tools long gone, but the albino managed to pull out two empty canteens—actually three, but one had a hole in the bottom—a spade with a broken handle, and a pickaxe in surprisingly good condition. He

also found an ear—a human ear—equally well pre-
served, which gave Whitey Grey great pleasure and
almost an hour of entertainment.

I cringed whenever he pointed the copper-colored
atrocity, coated with dust, at me, and Ian Spencer
Henry kept gagging, while Jasmine refused to show
any girlish emotion. Instead, she merely shook her
head to dismiss the albino's childishness.

"That's gross!" Ian Spencer Henry said, ducking
his head as Whitey Grey swept the ear toward him.
"Don't put that thing near me!"

"What's that, boy?" The white-skinned man
howled. "Speak up, kid. This Apache can't hear too
good!"

"Apache?" I asked, curious now instead of re-
pulsed.

"Yeah." Whitey Grey flipped the ear as he might a
two-bit piece, caught it, studied it. "I bet the gent
who earned this trophy is upset he lost it."

"Do you think it's from one of those Indians who
left San Carlos?" asked Ian Spencer Henry, keeping
his distance from the ear.

The albino snorted. "No, by grab, this might've
got took 'bout the time that bluecoat capt'n got kilt
here. Placed is name after him, you know. That was
in the 'Seventies. Maybe this here ear gots took afore
that. Desert has a way with bodies. Preserves 'em
good, you see, iffen the coyotes and the wolves and
the ravens don't gets at 'em."

Sticking the grisly trophy in his pocket, he wandered over to the Sheffield velocipedes to check
the tool boxes. "Let's see," he said, "if there's somethin' better for us here. We'll take 'em two canteens with us, fill 'em at the water hole afore we
enter the cañon."

Whispered Ian Spencer Henry urgently: "He's not going to kill us."

"Shut up," Jasmine snapped. "He might hear us."

Yet we had nothing to fear from the albino, for he pulled out a bottle of mescal, about three-quarters full, from the small box, and cut loose with a Rebel yell. "Praise be!" he yelled, holding the bottle high over his head. "And my flask was empty!"

By dusk, Whitey Grey was roostered. By the time the moon had risen, he was stretched out underneath the false water tower, Winchester at his side, empty bottle smashed on the rocks in front of him, singing at the top of his lungs.

Sittin' by the roadside on a summer day,
Chattin' with my messmates, passin' time away,
Lyin' in the shadow underneath the trees,
Goodness, how delicious, eatin' goober peas!
Peas! Peas! Peas! Peas! Eatin' goober peas!
Goodness, how delicious, eatin' goober peas!

For some reason, Ian Spencer Henry thought this might be a good time to carry on a conversation with the drunkard.

"You lived in Detroit, I heard you say. How long?"

"Five years," he said, and sang: "Five delicious years. Chattin' with my messmates, passin' time away."

"I'd like to visit all the big cities," Ian Spencer Henry informed him. "And Michigan's where. . . ."

"And I've seen 'em all," Whitey Grey said. "All the big ones. Detroit. Huntsville. Jefferson City." He sang again: "Goodness, how delicious, eatin' goober peas."

"Keep talking to him," I told my friend, and slowly rose. Jasmine sat up straighter, staring at me as I crept toward the rocks, listening to Whitey Grey sing and talk, listening to Ian Spencer Henry, now that he had a chore to do, stumble at asking anything. Jasmine had to assist him.

The three of us might be able to move the velocipede cars onto the track, heading east, away from Whitey Grey and Doubtful Cañon. Despite rolling clouds, the moon, practically full, would be bright enough, and, besides, a coal oil headlamp was affixed at the front. Just make sure we didn't pinch off a finger trying to put the flanged wheels on the rails. Ride as fast as we could, get back to Lordsburg, reconsider our options there, in relative safety.

I touched the metal bar, still warm from the day's sun, and jumped at a *thump* behind me.

"It's us, Jack!" Jasmine said in a whisper.

I blinked, stammered, looking for Whitey Grey to come charging, shooting.

"It's all right," Ian Spencer Henry said. "He's snorin' like a freight train. That fool drunk. . . ." He stopped, his face apologetic.

"What are you doing, Jack?" Jasmine asked.

Before I could reveal my plan, a wolf howled. An owl answered.

"I'm scared, Jack," Jasmine said.

"Jasmine, that's just. . . ." Ian Spencer Henry couldn't finish. Silence returned except for the albino's drunken snores, and a terrible thought raced through my mind.

Animals . . . or Apaches?

"He . . . Mister Grey . . . he says that Apaches don't attack at night," Jasmine said.

As if mocking her, the wolf howled again.

Maybe, I thought. Yet we'd make enough noise to wake the dead trying to move those Sheffield velocipedes back on the tracks, and, even if the Apaches didn't attack us, they might learn our position. On the other hand, they might have heard Whitey Grey's drunken singing. Or maybe they didn't know we were here. Maybe those were wolves and owls and not Indians. Maybe Whitey Grey would wake up, find us, kill us. Maybe we couldn't move those vehicles to the tracks. If we did, maybe a train would run us down and kill us. Maybe I didn't want to go home, to face my father. Maybe. . . .

"Too many things might go wrong," I said, once more plagued by doubts.

"What do you mean?" Jasmine asked. "What are you talking about?"

It hit me that I hadn't told them my thinking, but now it didn't matter. Right or wrong, I had made the decision to stay.

"I'll take first watch," I announced. Back underneath the tower, I picked up the Winchester and wandered back to the rocks, made myself as comfortable as possible, and watched the haunting moon creeping between clouds across the black sky.

The rifle jerked from my hands, and I let out a sharp cry, trying to stand, but a rough hand shoved me back, and the shriek of an Indian warrior pierced my ears.

My cry turned into a scream, and the next thing I heard was Whitey Grey laughing.

He tossed the rifle to his left hand, stuck out his right, and pulled me to my feet. My face reddened from embarrassment.

Dawn. No, well past dawn. I had fallen asleep

during my watch. Some help! Should I have taken that chance, tried to turn the railroad vehicles around, and escaped? Regrets filled my mind.

"You didn't get cold?" the albino asked.

I shrugged. I had been too tired to notice.

"Well, that's a good lad, Jack Dunivan. Takin' watch like that. I must've been plumb tuckered out. A fine pard you showed yourself to be. Yes, sir. That's somethin' I like in my pardner. Make me proud, it does. You gots the makin's of a fine man."

Oddly my embarrassment and loathing faded, replaced by a curious feeling of pride.

Leaning the rifle on the rocks, Whitey Grey reached over and tilted my head up so I stared into his wild eyes, which now looked friendly. "I like you, Jack Dunivan. You're a man to ride the river with, sure 'nough. Now, here's somethin' I was meanin' to do yesterday."

His callused fingers gripped my broken nose, and with a grunt and snort, in one sudden motion, he set it before I realized his intentions. Almost simultaneously, my eyes tearing from pain, my nose bleeding again, I let out a yell and a vile oath I had heard Whitey Grey use a couple of times.

"There." My pard stepped back, examining his medical work and nodding with satisfaction. " 'Tain't so crooked now."

Chapter Ten

"What about breakfast?" Ian Spencer Henry demanded.

Thought of food made the albino, suddenly looking paler than ever, groan, but he wasn't the only one hurting. I took Jasmine's proffered handkerchief and dabbed my nose.

"My belly's tetchy," Whitey Grey said. "Y'all et yesterday. Grub in your gut now'll just slow us down."

"No," Jasmine said. "We didn't eat yesterday. We haven't eaten since supper the night we left."

Upon realization on this fact, my stomach began to grumble, even louder than Whitey Grey's complaints, and I forgot all about my nose. Through bloodshot eyes, he stared at each of us, and perhaps reading a mutiny if we didn't get something to eat, he exhaled and pointed at the Sheffield velocipedes. "Well, 'tain't no Drover's Cottage, 'tain't no Texas Hotel, or my ma's fried taters, but I recollect there bein' some crackers and maybe an airtight in that tool box on that centipede car. Fill your bellies, chil'ren ... reckon you do need some strength to haul out all that gold we's gonna get ... 'cause it's a hard walk from here." He sighed again. "Wisht I had some coffee," he said. "Better yet, a mornin' bracer of rye."

I detested canned tomatoes, hated tomatoes of any kind, and the crackers were stale, but Ian Spencer Henry, Jasmine, and I savored the railroaders' left-over food as if we were dining at a Shakespeare social on Thanksgiving. We even found a piece of cured ham, which must have fallen off a sandwich and smelled more of oil and dust than pork, but we divided it into three pieces and ate it as well, washing breakfast down with the last of the water from Ian Spencer Henry's canteen. We'd have to make it those six or so miles to the water hole with dry throats, but, with our appetites appeased, we didn't seem to mind.

Nor did we consider the fact that Whitey Grey, mastermind of this campaign, had brought no food. Perhaps he planned on shooting game, living off the land, although around Stein's Peak—they pronounced it Steens—we didn't find a whole lot to live on. No horses or mules, either. Had he planned on walking into the cañon, digging up the gold, and returning to the railroad tracks afoot? Were horses waiting for us at the old Butterfield station? Did he even have a plan? These thoughts would come to me on the long, arid walk north.

I wiped my mouth with the back of my hand. Whitey Grey stood, rifle butted on the ground, staring at the rugged peak named after the Army officer killed here by Apaches back in 1973. My nose had stopped bleeding, and I handed the handkerchief to Jasmine, who looked at the stains and shook her head.

"That's all right, Jack. You keep it."

"Let's get movin'," Whitey Grey said, "afore the sun gets much higher."

We walked along an old road, kicking up dust,

trailing the albino who moved with an urgency, yet with caution. Sometimes Whitey Grey struck me as pure fool, but now he reminded me more of some great Western hero.

"He's like Kit Carson," Ian Spencer Henry said. "I was reading about him in *The Prince of the Gold Hunters*. It's an old one, but, gosh, it's full of blood and thunder and killings and treasure and excitement."

A thought struck me. I hadn't had time to ask him about it since our adventures began after we plunged off that train at Lordsburg. "Is that why you were late?"

Looking at his dusty boots, he kicked a rock in front of him as we walked. "Well . . . yeah." He laughed. "But I was learning about hunting gold from that story. It was like one of our school assignments you give me and Jasmine."

"You almost got left behind." I remembered something else, the pain and frightful experience of tumbling beside a speeding train. "You almost got Jasmine and me run over. By thunder, we could have broken our necks. Or got chopped to pieces."

"Well. . . ." He kicked another loose stone in front of us.

"And why did you run away?" My anger began to boil over. "When Mister Grey had that row with the railroad workers, when he was about to murder them? You took off running south. Deserted Jasmine and me."

"I was scared," he said honestly.

My fists clenched. My face flushed, yet Ian Spencer Henry cooled my rising anger with a reminder. "But I come back, Jack. Remember? I ran back and kept that wild man from killing you and Jasmine. Remember?"

"I remember," I said, suddenly ashamed of myself. "Why'd you come back? You could have been killed jumping on Mister Grey like you did."

Another rock danced up the road in front of us, propelled by Ian Spencer Henry's foot. "By jingo, Jack, what a fool question. *Because we're friends.*"

That said it all. I reached over and parted Ian Spencer Henry's back.

"Stop that chatter, chil'ren," Whitey Grey said. "You'll just swallow dust and alert any bushwhackers or Cherry Cows that we's comin'."

The rest of the journey we made in silence, the only noise coming from our footfalls and the rattling of the empty canteens bouncing against our thighs and the makeshift pack the albino had manufactured back at Stein's Peak station. In it we carried the broken-handled spade, other odds and ends including the albino's plunder, plus Ian Spencer Henry's was bag, with the pickaxe fastened outside. We took turns carrying the pack of our backs. Well, by we, I mean Ian Spencer Henry, Jasmine and me, not Whitey Grey.

Wind and sun had scorched the earth, shadowed by the nigh 6,000-foot-high peak now southwest of us. The only vegetation to be found came from century plants scattered along the side of the road. By the time we reached the small hollow, my lips had cracked, my mouth felt like sand, and my feet had begun to blister. Relief washed over me when Whitey Grey announced: "There she is."

It didn't last long.

"Where's . . . what?" Jasmine asked.

"The Overland station," the albino answered, quickening his pace. "Just like I remembers it."

Whitey Grey had some imagination, for all I found

were ancient, charred ruins and crumbling rock and adobe walls, mostly foundation. To here men like Whitey Grey and Mr. John Eversen talk, Stein's Peak station bustled with the excitement of the Tucson depot, but I spotted only a few lizards. Walking along the old foundation, I guessed that the biggest part of the prison-like compound had been the corral. Two small rooms had once faced the west wall, no larger than eight-by-fifteen feet, and a smaller one in the southeastern corner of the corral. Outside the east wall, a lean-to had been rebuilt, and Jasmine, Ian Spencer Henry, and I took shelter underneath its roof corduroyed with agave stalks, tossing the backpack in a corner.

"Where's the well?" Jasmine asked. "I'm parched."

"The Apaches poisoned it," Ian Spencer Henry answered. "Remember his story?" His jaw jutted out toward Whitey Grey, who shifted his rifle to one hand and asked us to hand him the canteens.

"You chil'ren looks tuckered out," he said with a grin, his hangover gone. "I'll get us something' to drink."

"But," I said, "the well . . . the Apaches. . . ."

"Well dried up years ago, I reckon, after the Apaches done their dirty deed back in 'Sixty-One. Used to be 'neath 'em dead cottonwoods. But they's a spring just west of here, inside the cañon." He gathered the canteens. "Be back in a jiffy."

I watched him go, crossing a sunburned meadow and heading toward rising hills dotted with a handful of juniper, an arrow-shaped rock (well, a crooked arrow, maybe) jutting toward the peak. Whitey Grey walked easily until the county swallowed him up.

Heavy panting woke me, and I sat up suddenly. "Hush now," the frantic albino was saying, his rough hands shaking Ian Spencer Henry and Jasmine from their slumbers. "Ol' Whitey Grey found a peck of trouble."

"What?" I rubbed my eyes.

"Quiet," His left hand shot toward me, holding a canteen. "Take a drink of that, and pass it 'round. Don't drink too much."

As we slaked our thirsts, the wiry man crawled to the edge of the crumbling foundation and peered toward the cañon entrance. "Saw Apache sign all over down yonder," he whispered. "What's more, some fool up and tried to build a house just beyond the spring. Rock house. Right comfy. But there ain't been a body there in some time, I warrant. Maybe, Nana likely drove 'em out of there, or maybe Cochise. Don't matter none."

"Should we go back?" Jasmine asked. "Back home?"

"Not without my gold," he answered. "Ain't got time nohow, because that ain't all I seen by the spring and in that house and all. No, sir. Seen petticoat sigh." Swearing, he lifted himself up on his elbows.

I took another mouthful, swallowed, handed the canteen to Jasmine. "Mister Gidding's daughter?" I said.

"Yeah. Likely. After my gold!" He lowered himself and backed into the lean-to, sat up, and unscrewed another canteen. After drinking greedily, he collected all the canteens and tilted his head toward the cañon.

"See that pointy rock? That's where we's goin'. I wants you to run, keep in a crouch, and move 'bout like you was a snake, goin' this way, then t'uther. Keep, say, thirty rods betwixt you. Make it difficult for any Apache to shoot you down. You first, Jack, ol' pard. Run like the wind! But, here, don't forget our possibles." He reached for the pack.

I made no effort to rise, for my legs didn't want to co-operate, and I couldn't blame them. "Do . . . do you see . . . any . . . Apaches out there?" I asked.

"Don't see nothin' now. Which makes me wary. Now, go, pard. More places to hide in that cañon than in this lean-to."

That made sense, and, forgetting all about my sore feet, I rose, letting the albino help secure the pack over my shoulders, then ducked, turned, and sprinted for my life, zigging and zagging, darting, legs pounding, pickaxe, shovel, and everything else rattling noisily, taking in huge gulps of air through my mouth. Twice I stumbled, but maintained my footing, watching the sharp rock draw closer, hearing the footsteps of Jasmine Allison and Ian Spencer Henry behind me. Breathlessly I reached the rugged rock and hugged it, let the backpack fall to the dirt. Moments later, Jasmine joined me, and soon Ian Spencer Henry arrived. Sinking to our knees, we heaved, wetting our lips, watching the albino snake his way across the meadow floor. Only he didn't stop at the rock. He kept going . . . into Doubtful Cañon.

"C'mon, chil'ren," he said. "Keep close, and keep your eyes peeled for that thievin' hussy!"

We moved silently, close together now, sweating although it wasn't hot, frightened by every shadow, every singing cicada, every scurrying lizard. The land opened for about a mile, maybe a mile and a half, into a gentle meadow, and Whitey Grey pointed out the spring and the rock ranch house he had discovered, buttressing the walls, door open heavy wooden shutters closed. The building lacked warmth, reminding me more of a deathtrap, and I could see why it would be abandoned with Apaches on the loose.

Yet it looked much more inviting than the cañon, which turned treacherous as the meadow narrowed and descended into the cooling depths of the desert, dark rock walls rising until they towered over us. I felt as if I were walking into a grave. My grave. Our grave.

With caution, we moved westward, hugging the north wall, dodging boulders, hiding behind juniper, side-stepping cactus. Shadows lengthened, and we stopped to rest, sitting beside a rock cairn while Whitey Grey scouted a few rods ahead before returning a moment later.

His eyes blazed with recognition, and suddenly the albino smiled, pointing at the rocks upon which we rested.

"Hey, that's where we buried Sam Golden and the Mex. Buried what was left of 'em, I mean." We leaped off the grave, brushing dirt off our backsides, prompting a short burst of laughter from the white-skinned man. "Nothin' to fear, chil'ren. You ain't gonna wake 'em up. Let's go."

Above us, the rock walls stretched skyward, and I recalled stories of Apaches rolling boulders from the bluffs, crushing their trapped enemies to death. The canvas pack on my back felt much, much heavier. No longer could I see the sun, and the air had turned much cooler. The wind picked up, howling among strewn boulders, whistling through junipers and brush. We'd walk, wait, listen, creep along the cañon edge for a few yards, and wait again, sometimes as long as five or ten minutes.

Whitey Grey leaned his rifle, hammer pulled back to full cock, against a dead juniper, wiped his palms on his filthy britches, and slowly pulled the Colt from his waistband. Quietly he blew on the cylinder, spun it, then held the weapon out, butt forward.

"You know how to shoot this thing?" he asked.

Blinking, I fought back disappointment.

"Sure," Jasmine answered.

"Kicks like a lady dancin' the cancan," he said. "And they's six beans in the wheel. Some fools think it's safer to keep the hole 'neath the hammer empty, but 'tain't safe, iffen you asks me. That's carelessness." As soon as Jasmine held the six-shooter, the gun shaking in her two small hands, Whitey Grey picked up the Winchester, told us to stay put, and disappeared in the thick forest of fallen rocks and dirt before us.

A hawk's shrill cry echoed across the cañon. Jasmine aimed the wobbling Colt at the far side of the cañon. Unwilling to be out here unarmed, I picked up a good-size stone. Beside me, Ian Spencer Henry brought out a slingshot he had managed to keep hidden the past two days.

A dove *cooed*, and Ian Spencer Henry stepped forward.

"What are you doing?" I asked hoarsely.

"That's Mister Grey's signal," he replied. "Safe to come. Let's catch up with him, get that gold, get out of here."

"How . . . ?"

My friend grinned. "Read about it in *Prince of the*

Gold Hunters. I told you I was studying. Here, Jack, it's my turn with the pack. Let me carry it."

Reluctantly we followed, but it turned out Ian Spencer Henry was right. The albino's head bobbed with approval, and we inched our way through the thickening, deepening, widening cañon, armed with Winchester, Colt, slingshot, and rock. The walls closed in on us.

Slipping the canvas pack off his shoulders, Ian Spencer Henry peered ahead, stepped back, and said: "Gosh a'mighty. Is that Mister Giddings's body?"

Whirling, the white-skinned man stared ahead, and Jasmine and I rushed beside him for a better view. Staked out in the middle of the road lay a body in buckskins and muslin, pinned by at least two dozen arrows, the sand all around him blackened by blood. His head faced us, mouth open as if screaming—and I could almost hear his pitiful cries—his eyes . . . *missing.* His boots were gone, too, leaving a sock on his left foot, big toe protruding from a hole.

Quickly Jasmine looked away, making the sign of the cross, while I fought down rising bile and dropped my rock.

"Giddings?" Whitey Grey gave Ian Spencer Henry a look of bewilderment, uncertainly.

"You said the desert here preserves a body," my friend explained. "Like the Apache ear you took from that shed. Is that Mister Giddings?"

Again the albino blinked. His left hand fished the ear from his pocket, returned it, and he bit his bottom lip, his face masked in confusion, turned back to consider the mutilated body fifteen yards away.

Whitey Grey cleared his throat. "Mister Giddings?" he called out and sank back behind the rocks.

No answer, except his haunting echo. The albino looked even more puzzled. So did I, but it was Whitey Grey who baffled me. *Did he think a dead man could answer him?*

Poor Jasmine Allison just looked sick.

A full minute stretched before Whitey Grey rose to study the corpse again. His pale head shook, he sank back onto his haunches, and he started mumbling, more to himself than to answer Ian Spencer Henry. "No. No. Can't be. We buried Giddings, what was left of him anyway, bones and all. No, that ain't Mister Giddings. He's dead. I seen him die. I practically kilt. . . ." He shut up, gripping the Winchester tightly, eyebrows lowering, his face registering fear.

"Apaches is amongst us!" he screamed, his voice echoing like a choir in a cave, and he ran, crossing the small passageway, hurdling the arrow-filled body, darting for the other wall.

Chapter Eleven

The wind began to howl, kicking up a brief but violent dust devil that lashed out against a fortification of granite boulders, behind which hid three shaking children and one albino adult.

Ian Spencer Henry, Jasmine, and I had raced after our fleeing leader, finding shelter on the far side of the narrow cañon, although what made it a better spot than the other side, we would remain clueless. When the wind abated, or maybe after we had survived ten or fifteen minutes without being killed, Whitey Grey's mettle returned.

"This was the spot," he said, looking up, his voice quiet in reflection. "Too narrow to turn a Concord, turn anythin' 'round." Lacking mirth, he laughed. " 'Long 'bout here's where it all happened. I recollect it fine, picture it." He pointed toward the road's edge. "There's where the Concord got wrecked." Pointed again to a clearing. "Over yonder's where Mister Giddings got laid low. We buried him . . . yonder."

"We should bury him, too." I gestured toward the eyeless corpse.

"Bury 'im?" The white-skinned man snorted in derision, his voice, like his courage, rising a few levels. "With Apaches amongst us?"

"Yeah," said Ian Spencer Henry, angering me by siding with the white-skinned man. "Besides, I left the pack with the shovel and pick over there."

"You done what?" The albino looked angry, then sickened as he stared across the cañon floor. Sure enough, Whitey Grey's makeshift pack leaned against a twisted alligator juniper, handle to the pickaxe sprouting up like a pale tree. Our leader groaned. "Son, son, son," he said, "we'll have need of that pick and shovel."

"And my pistol," Ian Spencer Henry added. "I brought along Pa's old Navy Colt. It's in my war bag. I remember how much you said you liked your old Navy, it being the weapon of your choice. And I've read that Wild Bill preferred it, as well."

"Lots of good it done him," said Whitey Grey, taking his revolver from Jasmine's quaking hands and shoving it into his waistband. "And lots of good that shovel and pick's gonna do us settin' over yonder. Might need 'em to gets my gold. Will need 'em." He glared at Ian Spencer Henry. "Go fetch 'em, boy."

"But . . . but . . . but. . . ." My friend sought help, and, finding none, said: "But it was Jasmine's turn to carry the pack. She should go."

Whitey Grey was not swayed. "You're goin'."

"But . . . but there are Apaches all over."

"Likely not," he said. "Else they'd have cut one or two of you chil'ren down whilst you crossed the cañon."

"But you said we're surrounded by Apaches. More or less, you said it."

"Been wrong. Let's see iffen I'm wrong now."

Ian Spencer Henry tried to argue further, but Whitey Grey's patience had limits, so I laid my canteen on the ground, slid through the opening between the rocks, and made my way across the old Overland road.

"Jack!" Jasmine yelled. "Don't . . . !"

I didn't listen, just kept walking, sure to feel an arrow slice into my heart at any second. Silence returned. I could feel the anxious stares of Whitey Grey, Ian Spencer Henry, and Jasmine Allison boring through my back as I moved slowly, not quite deliberately. Don't cite my action as bravery. One of us had to get those tools, and I owed Ian Spencer Henry. Yes, he had irritated me a minute earlier, but I couldn't forget all he had done in the past. Back along the Southern Pacific tracks, he had charged out of the desert, maybe stopping the wild man named Whitey Grey from killing me, and he had been my friend, a true friend, since I had known him. In the desert, he had shared his water with Jasmine and me. Besides, Ian Spencer Henry hadn't gotten us into this mess. Back in Shakespeare, had I said no, had I told them we were not running away with a man we did not know chasing gold we did not know existed, we wouldn't be in such a predicament. If anyone needed to cross the road, as bait for Apaches, it had to be me.

One mistake almost cost me my breakfast. As I walked past the dead man, I looked down at him. I had seen his face from a distance, the darkened, bloody holes where his eyes had been, the mouth locked in an eternal scream, but distance is one thing. Up close, with the fear of an imminent Apache attack palatable, that's something entirely different. He hadn't been scalped—Apaches weren't prone to such depredations—probably not even tortured, but I could not think of death coming in a more gruesome fashion. Once I'd read a newspaper description of a body killed by Indians in which the writer said the dead man resembled a porcupine or pin-cushion, but those allusions do an injustice.

This was once a man?

I swallowed, took a deep breath, let the dizziness pass, went on.

Would I soon join him?

Nothing happened. To my surprise, I reached the canvas pack where Ian Spencer Henry had left it. Struggling with the weight, though it wasn't that heavy, I pulled the strap to my left shoulder, hefted it, kept my right hand free, and began the walk back, not far in a physical sense but stretching infinite miles in my beleaguered mind.

Just put one foot in front of the other, I told myself. *There's nothing you can do now anyway. If they kill you, they kill you. Destiny's not something you control, Jack Dunivan. Walk. Walk. It's the easiest thing in the world to do. You've been doing it for eleven years.*

"That a boy, pard. You's almost here. Good lad, Jack Dunivan, good lad."

My eyes opened. Apparently I had closed them for ten or twelve rods. Now I again saw the remains of Willie Spoon; at least I assumed the dead man to be the guide from Lordsburg.

"Don't look at him, Jack," Jasmine said. "Don't stop." Her eyes widened in terror, wonderment, be-wilderment, something. "Jack . . . what on earth?"

Leaning down, I grabbed the collar of the dead man's muslin shirt, and, with a grunt, I heaved, surprised at my strength. The arrows, those that had driven through the man's body, snapped at their ends. Maybe Willie Spoon didn't weigh much, for he certainly looked small in death, or maybe men are as light as air once life leaves them. Maybe

I summoned up some force of energy through my own fear. I gave another yank, squatting, pulling, dragging him toward our makeshift fort.

"Boy," Whitey Grey said, "don't bring 'im in here." He sounded like a child, scared of the dead.

"Gross," said Ian Spencer Henry.

No one offered to assist me, even when it became clear that the Apaches wouldn't kill me, and I didn't blame them. Turning sideways, I managed to slide through the rock opening, tossing the pack and tools at Whitey Grey's feet, then reached back with both hands and dragged the dead man inside, too, arrows breaking in the rocks, shafts tearing at his body, but he was beyond hurting. Letting him drop, I collapsed, trying to catch my breath, fighting the distress in my chest and bowels.

"Gross," Ian Spencer Henry repeated, but kept staring at the remains. Jasmine looked away. Whitey Grey stared at me with rage.

"Did Apaches do that?" My friend pointed at the face.

"Ravens, I suspect," the white-skinned man said without looking away from me. "We probably scairt 'em off. Or the Cherry Cows give 'em birds a fright."

"Gross," Ian Spencer Henry said again, and looked at me. "What did you bring him here for, Jack? He's dead. Nothing we can do for him."

"We can bury him," I said. "We can bury him if we're decent people." Now I was looking into Whitey Grey's soulless eyes. "You owe him that much, don't you, Mister Grey?" I pointed at the corpse, although now I could not summon up courage to look into the dead man's face again, or his bloodied body. "You remember him, sir, for he remembered you. Willie

Spoon? He was freighting with that group that found you at the station twenty years ago. If not for him, and all those others with him, the Apaches might have killed you, or you would have starved to death at the old Overland station. Then you'd be buried, along with Mister Giddings and those others killed by the Apaches."

"Over yonder then." The albino pointed to the small clearing. "Where we buried Mister Giddings and poor ol' Bruce from Wisconsin way." He grinned. "Give 'em Cherry Cows one more chance to kill you."

"Fine," I said, no longer believing Indians remained in the vicinity. I opened the pack, grabbed the shovel with the broken handle, loosened the rawhide thongs securing the pickaxe, and walked to the unmarked graves.

"Here," Ian Spencer Henry said. "I'll join you, Jack. Let me help."

"Me, too," Jasmine said.

The albino just swore, found a spot in the shade, and rolled a cigarette.

We dug near the two graves, not that you could tell this was a cemetery of sorts. The freighters had been in a hurry to bury Mr. Giddings and the other man. The rocks they had piled over the shallow graves had been scattered here and there after two decades. If any cross or other marker had ever been erected, and I doubted they had, they, too, had been washed, blown, or ripped away.

Jasmine swung the pickaxe with the fury of a Shakespeare miner. I worked the shovel, ignoring the blisters forming on my hands, scraping more than digging, not making much progress in the hard earth. Having fished out a wooden box from his war bag, Ian Spencer Henry stood guard.

He had pulled a .44 Colt from the box, proudly showing it off to an unimpressed Whitey Grey, who merely said: " 'Taint a Navy, boy, but an Army. Careful not to blow off your hand shootin' it."

Once, the Army Colt had been impressive, its nickel plating ornately engraved though now dotted with flakes of rust, the brass pieces tarnished green, the checkered ivory grip faded to a mellow yellow. The box also contained a copper flask upon which, under a coat of dust, were engraved scenes of a cannon, balls, and flags, with crossed muskets at the top, and a bullet mold. A tin of percussion caps lay in one corner, and other caps had spilled out, and Ian Spencer Henry pulled out a box of prefabricated paper cartridges and loaded the revolver, or tried to, for most of the old, antiquated cartridge fell apart before ever reaching the cylinder, spilling ancient black powder into the dust. Yet he had managed to get three cartridges and caps in place, and proudly stood in the shadows, protecting us.

Oh, Ian Spencer Henry would come to our assistance when needed, shoving the Colt into his waistband and helping Jasmine pry loose the pickaxe, kicking rocks and mounds of dirt out of the way, even offering to spell me while I nursed the blisters.

Which is more than Whitey Grey did. He just stood several yards away in the corner, Winchester in his arms, Colt on a boulder top within easy reach, eyes searching the cañon rim.

With dusk approaching, and bedrock refusing to bend to our muscles, I announced the grave sufficient, though we had not even reached a depth of two feet, and we retrieved the corpse.

"Good," Whitey Grey said. "Y'all be his pall-bearers."

"You should say something over his grave," Jasmine said.

He considered this for a moment, looking again up and down the cañon, and his head bobbed, which surprised me. "Reckon that'd be all right," he said, and, picking up his Colt and rifle, followed us as Jasmine, Ian Spencer Henry, and I dragged the dead man to his final resting place. We didn't look at the body, and, when he tumbled into the pit face down, no one volunteered to roll him over.

"No need to, chil'ren," the albino said. "Let the ol' hand alone. He's tellin' the Apaches what he thinks of 'em." And he laughed, this time with humor, although we found nothing funny.

I removed the Irish woolen hat, too large for me anyway, that Whitey Grey had procured, and bowed my head, waiting for the strange man's eulogy and prayer.

He kept it brief.

"We commit his body to the deep in the certain . . . oh, amen. Scrape some sand o'er 'em, chil'ren, and let's go gets my gold. I think it's up yonder way." He pointed catty-corner from us, and stepped back while Ian Spencer Henry and I, as soon as we had recovered from the albino's actions, began covering the remains of the late Willie Spoon.

"I wonder what happened to Miss Giddings," Jasmine said to no one in particular.

"She's worser off than that ol' boy," Whitey Grey answered. "But at least she's out of my territory, away from my gold."

"That's a cruel thing to say," Jasmine snapped back.

"She was warned, li'l' girlie. Railroaders told her Doubtful Cañon ain't no place for no petticoat. Just be thankful 'em Apaches who done that, or 'em who wisht they had done it, ain't 'round here no more."

His words had barely registered when death knocked me senseless.

I lay sprawled on my back, fighting for breath, the broken-handled spade knocked somewhere in the cactus. Instinctively I reached out, grabbed a hand, forced my eyes open, and stared into the blackest, cruelest eyes I had ever seen.

"Look outs, chil'ren!" Whitey Grey screamed. A gunshot roared. "Blast my luck, they's here. The Apaches is here!"

Another shot.

I gasped. The hand I held gripped a huge bone-handled knife with one wicked blade inches from my throat.

He had not screamed some blood-curdling yell, had merely fallen from the sky, it seemed, and landed on me. His face was copper, mouth closed, eyes venomous, shiny black hair hanging to his shoulders, and a scarlet silk headband across his forehead, his cheeks plastered with grains of sand I could make out clearly. He stank of sweat, of buckskins and grease. The blade lowered.

"No you don't," I said, or tried to say. "You're not killing me!"

Another weapon *boomed*. Hoofs. My ears rang. Shouts now, like coyotes yipping.

"Shoot him!" It was Jasmine's voice. "Shoot him."

With what? I don't have a gun. My mind worked

briefly. She wasn't talking to me, but urging Ian Spencer Henry to save my life.

What's taking you so long? I thought, wanting to seek out my good friend, wanting to see that Ian Spencer Henry would indeed save my life, but I remained scared witless to take my eyes away from the Apache on top of me. *Kit Carson, Buffalo Bill, Deadwood Dick . . . they'd have sent this man to Glory by now, Ian Spencer Henry!*

Man? No. Why he was nothing more than a boy, maybe my age, no more than a year or two older.

Another shot. Then a succession, a veritable cannonade. Whitey Grey's Winchester sent round after round at our attackers, but the albino didn't notice the fix I was in, or had enough trouble himself.

I heard the *click*, then another, followed by a curse from Ian Spencer Henry. "My gun ain't working!" he yelled. "Confound it!"

Isn't working, Ian Spencer Henry. There's no such word as ain't.

Would those be my last thoughts?

Jasmine soared, hit the young Apache, but he flung her off effortlessly. Another gunshot. Ian Spencer Henry gave a shout, slammed the revolver barrel at the Apache's head, missing when he ducked, and hit his shoulder instead. Bone crunched, and the Apache groaned, the first emotion to register on his face other than a grim, deadly determination to rid the world of me.

His grip relaxed, and I forced the knife up and away, but he roared in pain and rage, and the blade came down savagely. I ducked, felt the knife slide past my ear, slam into the ground. The Apache muttered something, and Ian Spencer Henry and

Jasmine hit him again. He let go of me to fight them, and my right hand shot out, searching for anything, jerking back from the stab of a yucca, but trying again, gripping something hard, wooden. . . . The spade! I brought it up, slammed the tool into the Apache's face, felt him cry out in pain and astonishment.

He fell backward, nose spurting blood.

Another bullet sang off the rocks.

The Apache boy rolled onto the unfinished grave, saw the corpse of Willie Spoon, and shrieked in terror. He bolted.

"Hey, you!" Whitey Grey yelled out, noticing the young warrior for the first time. He swung his Winchester, fired, missing, the bullet *spanging* off the boulders, shot again, but the Apache was gone, disappearing as mysteriously and as silently as he had arrived.

A bullet, one that hadn't been fired by Whitey Grey, kicked up sand to my right. I pulled up my knees, backed to the corner, tried to catch my breath, to slow my heart, fight down the panic. Ian Spencer Henry and Jasmine joined me, chests heaving, sweating. The albino fired again, his curses followed by . . . silence.

A deafening quietude that lasted an eternity of minutes.

"You chil'ren ain't dead?" he called out after the longest time.

Lying prone, Ian Spencer Henry, his Army .44 trembling in two outstretched hands, spit out sand but did not answer. Nor did Jasmine, squatting behind me, holding the knife the Apache boy had dropped. I still gripped the spade.

My mouth and throat refused to co-operate. All I could do was move my head, and that took effort.

"What do we do?" Jasmine's voice had returned.

Grimly thumbing cartridges into the rifle, the albino answered with a shake of his head. The wind began to wail again, or maybe the Apaches were singing a battle song, preparing for the kill.

Chapter Twelve

As stillness returned and shadows lengthened, we waited, too scared to move, but eventually I summoned enough strength to kick and push rocks and dirt until the grave was covered. I can't say I did this out of respect or decency. No, fear prompted my actions. The more I saw the back of the dead man's head, the more I pictured my own face in a grave, mouth open, eyes gone, dead.

A peregrine falcon soared overhead, disappeared in the gloaming, and the air turned frightfully cold as darkness, perhaps death, descended. We huddled together, the three of us, surprised when Ian Spencer Henry let out a sigh of relief, and slowly rose in the creeping darkness.

"Ian Spencer Henry . . . ," Jasmine pleaded.

"Indians don't attack at night," he explained. "Don't you remember nothing?"

Before I could protest, the albino had crawled over, startling us out of our wits. He had gathered the canvas pack, and passed a canteen while cautioning us not to drink too much. "Leave the pick-axe and that spade here, by ol' Willie Spoon's grave. Don't reckon 'em Cherry Cows'll touch it, but hide our tools near 'em graves, behind that yucca yonder.

Here." He drew his Colt, spinning it, offering it butt forward, not to Jasmine this time, but me.

It felt heavy in my hands.

"You want to swap, Jack?"

"No," I snapped at Ian Spencer Henry, who eyed the new model revolver with envy.

"Hush now," the albino said. "We're sneakin' out afore the moon rises. Think I tol' you chil'ren that Apaches ain't ones to attack in the dark. So let's *vamanos.*"

"Told you." Ian Spencer Henry stuck out his tongue.

Ignoring him, Jasmine asked our leader: "Where are we going?"

"To that stone house built at the cañon's edge near the spring. You boys done good, fightin' that buck like y'all done. You, too, li'l' girlie. I'd come to help you, but I was busy a mite."

"How many Apaches were there?" I asked.

"Can't tell. One's all it takes to bury you. We might've got some luck on our side 'cause of you, Jack Dunivan. It was you who come up with the idea to bury ol' Willie Spoon. Got a big fear of the dead, 'em Apaches do. That body in the grave spooked 'em, spooked that buck tryin' to cut your gullet, at least, and he might've gone and tol' his red-devil friends. Maybe they've cleared out."

"Then why leave?" Ian Spencer Henry asked.

"'Cause maybe they ain't. Can't read no Apache's mind. Could be they's in a hurry to get to Mexico. Could be they's spoilin' for a fight. I gots no strong desire to leave my gold, us bein' practically spittin' distance to it, but I gots a better desire to keep my hair. I know, Jack Dunivan, 'em bucks don't take scalps, so don't get smart with me ag'in. We can come back and digs up that buried treasure, but let's wait a spell. That ranch house be a better place for us to fort up than out here. Cherry Cows, mean as they are, they'd start rollin' down rocks on our heads, save their powder, lead, and arrows. Three graves is here already, and I'm in no hurry to join 'em. Don't y'all fret none, chil'ren, 'cause ol' Whitey Grey had to make this walk in the dark afore, back after Mister Giddings got kilt here twenty years ago. I knows where I'm goin'. So let's get goin'.'"

Snaking in the darkness, inching through juniper, rocks, and yucca, we moved back up Doubtful Cañon, waiting for the moon to rise, but clouds filled the air, keeping us cloaked in darkness and cold. The wind moaned. We neither saw nor heard any Indians, coming across only one Gila monster, scaring it off, before wolves began a frightful song.

There was no path, not along the rugged walls, and the rocks scratched my battered palms and knees, the branches of the alligator junipers shedding on my stolen hat, assaulting my nostrils, the bark carving my back. When the wolves stopped, a falcon *screeched*, and Whitey Grey stopped abruptly.

"'Tain't no bird, that was," he said softly, and sat up, silently pulling back the Winchester's hammer.

A minute passed. Five. Ten. A full half hour we sat in the cold as the wind picked up, slowly building intensity, bringing with it the rumble of thunder. Dark clouds blackened the moon, and the dam burst.

Rain, brutally icy, fell in torrents, stinging like knives, soaking our clothes until we trembled.

"Glory be," Whitey Grey said, lowering the rifle's hammer. "Let's make a beeline, chil'ren." Lightning arced over the cañon, followed by a bellowing of thunder, and the white-skinned man ran, slipping, boots splashing in the mud. Cold and miserable, we followed, trying to keep up with him. We'd fall into blackness and wait, listening but hearing nothing now but the ferocity of the storm, waiting for that flash of lightning to reveal Whitey Grey's location. There. I'd see him, or Jasmine might spot him, and we'd stumble in the direction.

A boulder stung my hand, and my pinky finger throbbed in agony, and, when lightning struck so close our ears popped, Jasmine Allison tossed away her knife, warning us to do the same with our weapons. "I've heard of cowboys getting killed by lightning," she said, "striking their spurs and guns."

"My pa'll strike me dead if I lost his Colt," Ian Spencer Henry said. "He's gonna break out his razor strop, anyway, when he learns I took it, unless I share my sixteen hundred and sixty-six dollars and sixty-six cents. And I bet Mister Grey would frown upon you was you to shuck his gun into some puddle, Jack."

Lightning flashed again. "There!" I cried out, and pointed into the depths where I thought I'd spied Whitey Grey. "Let's go." I took the lead, keeping the Colt in my right hand. Lightning didn't scare me half as much as being caught in a cañon by Apaches, or being left in the desert alone. We ran after Whitey Grey.

After a few minutes, the rain slackened, and a moment later the storm had raged past us. By then, however, we had lost Whitey Grey, and without the benefit of lightning, now well off in the distance, I held little hope of finding him again.

Instead, Whitey Grey found us.

"Hey, chil'ren!" his voice called out. "That be you?"

I answered him, and heard his joints popping, his breath heaving, a grunt, a curse, stones rolling, splashing in a puddle, then a larger splash. He stepped forward, reaching out, fumbling in the darkness, and patted my shoulder.

"How you feel?"

"F-f-f-f-ree-zing." Jasmine's teeth chattered. "I-I-I-I'm so cold."

"Yeah, I knows it, but that storm, maybe it drove 'em Cherry Cows away. Softened up the ground some, too. Make it easier for y'all to dig up my gold. C'mon. That ranch ain't much farther up the road."

Ian Spencer Henry saw the light first.

He whispered a warning, and the albino crouched, not believing at first, even asking Jasmine and me to verify the small flickering light on the far side of Doubtful Cañon.

A reddish-white glow flickered, almost like a lightning bug, vanished, came back, and hovered about for a moment. The light began to fade, but now I could make out my comrades better, could perceive Jasmine squatting on a patch of bear grass behind a dead mesquite, her dark hair drenched, her whole body trembling. Ian Spencer Henry aimed his Army Colt at the fading light, growing smaller and smaller, and Whitey Grey tugged, twisted, and chewed on his mustache. I could distinguish the cañon rocks from the outline of the ranch house, knew the small light came from there. Only I could see more now, and, looking up, I realized the clouds had parted, moving with the storm, and the moon bathed us in reddish-yellow light.

The white-skinned man noticed it, too. "Raidin'

moon," he said. "Comanch' moon, we called it back in Texas. Now, I don't know what 'em Cherry Cows think 'bout it, but 'tain't no place to be out of doors in Texas when the moon be like this."

"The light's gone." Ian Spencer Henry aimed the revolver barrel at empty, gray rocks.

"Th-th-that's . . . the . . . h-h-house," Jasmine said.

"Uhn-huh," Whitey Grey said, frowning.

"You don't. . . ." Ian Spencer Henry looked at our leader for help. "You don't think it's . . . it's a . . . ghost . . . do you?"

He didn't answer. I stared away from the moon, and studied the house in the rocks, waiting for the light to reappear; but it never did.

"Candle," I said at last. "It had to be a candle."

"Yeah." Ian Spencer Henry's head bobbed. "Candle. Yeah. But who was holding it? A ghost?"

Jasmine stopped her chattering teeth. "Maybe . . . the r-r-rancher came . . . b-b-back."

" 'Tain't likely," Whitey Grey said, but he sounded uncertain. "And Cherry Cows gots no use for candles. Ghosts, neither. No. . . ."

My body shivered. The moon slowly slid westward, swallowed briefly by a passing cloud, then emerging as the peregrine falcon cried out from the cañon walls.

"Let's hoof it, chil'ren," the albino said, and he took off running, slipping once on the wet granite, exploding with speed, crouching, running in a criss-cross motion toward the rock house. Fearing that the falcon was Apache rather than raptor, we followed.

Until a bullet *spanged* off the rocks near us.

Another round echoed through the dark, but I spotted the muzzle flash as I dived behind a shrub,

Jasmine sailing beside me, Ian Spencer Henry finding shelter by a boulder, and Whitey Grey scrambling behind a mound of dirt.

"Tarnation," Ian Spencer Henry said. "I think that rain ruint all the powder in my pistol."

A bullet whined overhead.

"Hey, you in the cabin!" Whitey Grey called out. "Stop shootin'. We's white men!" Another bullet, closer this time. "And a li'l girlie."

"Go away!"

I blinked away confusion and doubt. The voice came from the abandoned house we had passed that day. A woman's voice. Not Apache. Not even Mexican. Frightened, she had to be, but more than handy with the rifle, although she hadn't hit any of us yet.

"Listen . . ."

A round cut off Whitey Grey's protest; and he snorted, rolled over, and looked at Jasmine and me. "Petticoat," he said, and spat. "Worthless, miserable petticoat." Shaking his head, he hollered back at the cabin. "Woman, we's white, I tell you, and we just gots waylaid by Apaches up the cañon. There's a raidin' moon out, and I ain't aimin' to wait out here to gets a Cherry Cow arrow in my brisket. I said, let us come in there."

"Go away!" she yelled again, but didn't fire her rifle.

"Woman, you's rilin' me. Now start actin' hospitable. . . ."

The rifle shot clipped a mesquite branch near Whitey Grey.

Craning his neck, he scouted the territory between his position and the house and, a few minutes later, pointed the Winchester barrel at a rock corral to the left of the house.

"You chil'ren," he said, "you run to that ol' corral. Keep your heads down."

"What?" Jasmine demanded, no longer stuttering and shivering from the cold.

"You heard me. I tol' you I ramrod this outfit. Now run. 'Tain't likely that hussy'll shoot y'all down. Run. Run or, by grab, I'll start shootin' at you, and I ain't gonna miss."

When we didn't follow his orders fast enough, he brought the Winchester up and sent a bullet between Jasmine and me.

So we ran, prodded by another round from Whitey Grey that kicked up dirt behind us, stinging my legs. Ian Spencer Henry ran, too, cutting loose with his version of a Rebel yell. The woman screamed, but her shouts were lost in the accompanying gunfire. Yet she wasn't shooting at us, but at Whitey Grey, or where he had been. When I realized she wouldn't kill us, I looked back for the white-skinned man, but he had gone, vanished.

We dived behind the wall. My ears rang from the gunfire, and then, lying on my chest, fighting for breath, wet, cold and scared, I located the apparition that was Whitey Grey, a wild ghost flashing through boulders and juniper, charging, rifle in his arms, mouth open, releasing a much more fiendish battle cry than Ian Spencer Henry's as he dived through the front door.

A gunshot *boomed* inside, loud, violent with a finality in its report.

Then . . . nothing.

Rolling over, I shot a look of concern at my friends. Another cloud hid the moon. A twig scratched in the cañon walls above us, and, when the falcon cried out again, I couldn't wait any longer, and, scrambling to my feet, I darted for the stone house, crying out for my friends to follow me.

Follow me? Ian Spencer Henry passed me, screaming to Whitey Grey, assuming the white-skinned man hadn't been killed by the woman inside, that we were coming in, to hold his fire, not to shoot us, that Apaches were amongst us. I slackened my pace, just long enough to grab Jasmine's hand, and ran, crashing through the threshold and stumbling on the hard-packed earthen floor.

The moon reappeared, its eerie light stretching through the open window and door, and we saw Whitey Grey, two rifles in his hands, making sure we were alone, and we were.

Whitey Grey . . . Jasmine Allison . . . Ian Spencer Henry . . . me . . . and a woman cowering in the corner, bruised arms wrapped around drawn-up knees, rocking back and forth.

Her auburn hair resembled a pat rack's nest, frizzy, a tangled mess, her shoes scuffed and ripped, riding skirt caked in dried mud and grime, the sleeves of her blouse tattered. Though I had never seen her before, I knew her instantly.

"Miss Giddings?" I spoke softly.

Her eyes burned in recognition of her name, and she studied me curiously.

"Who are you?" Her voice sounded surprisingly calm.

"I'm Jack Dunivan. You don't know me. I. . . ."

"Fireplace'll work," Whitey Grey interrupted. "Got some wood inside, too. Let's get some heat in this pigsty. Warm us up. Dry 'em rain-soaked duds of our'n."

"But the Apaches . . . ," Ian Spencer Henry said.

"Cherry Cows knows we's here," he said. "Likely

Mex bandits and ever' other rascal this side of the border, after all that commotion." He kicked a can, grabbed it, held it in the moonlight. "Glory be. Arbuckles' coffee. Must've missed it when I was scoutin' this place earlier." He pried off the lid. "Plenty of grounds, too. No peppermint candy, but that's all right. We'll have us some breakfast afore sunup."

He ordered Ian Spencer Henry to tend the fire, tossed the coffee can to Jasmine, grabbed a rifle, its stock splintered by a bullet, off the floor, and squatted before the frightened woman. "I tol' you we was white. You kept on shootin'." He let the old-model Henry *clatter* at her feet. "You's plumb lucky I didn't kill you, petticoat or not. You is Giddings's daughter, ain't you?"

Her head bobbed slightly.

"You was with a feller named Spoon."

She looked away, shutting her eyes like a slamming door, and I studied the house, small but solid, with a heavy oaken door and window facing the cañon and another smaller window in the rear, each window equipped with oak or walnut shutters, all of them open, none barred. Had the woman thought to secure the door, she might have kept Whitey Grey at bay. Trash littered the floor, and I espied no furniture, just a pile of wood and a yellow candle resting on the top of an empty can of sugar. Jasmine busied herself pouring coffee into a battered pot, and I cringed, thinking that would be some awfully strong breakfast we'd be forced to drink.

Ian Spencer Henry begged me to help with the fire, and I started to go, but turned, glaring at Whitey Grey when he told Miss Giddings: "I buried Spoon." He hadn't done a lick of work, had watched while we had buried the old man. "What was left of him nohow. So you tell me this, girlie, what in the Sam Hill is you doin' in this god-forsaken country, and, after 'em Cherry Cows hit you, how'd you make it back here . . . alive?"

Chapter Thirteen

She didn't speak for an hour, not until the sky turned gray and birds began to sing, not until flames roared in the fireplace, not until Ian Spencer Henry placed a steaming cup of black coffee, the one cup we had—after Whitey Grey had drunk his fill, of course—into her hands, not until Jasmine had given her a smile of encouragement. She sighed briefly, told us her name was Eleora, and tested the bitter brew. "Tell us, girlie," Whitey Grey said, softer, gentler this time, and moved to the door, Winchester cradled in his arms, peering outside.

"I . . . I never knew my father," Eleora Giddings began. "I. . . ." Tears streamed down her face, but only for a moment. Resolutely she brushed them away with a torn strip of cloth. Another sip of coffee fortified her, and she tried again.

This is the story the petrified woman told:

I wasn't even born when he left El Paso, I mean, well, it was Franklin back then. Called Franklin, I mean. Mama said she got word, two or three weeks later, that Papa had been killed by the Apaches on his trip to California, that he had died in a cañon somewhere in New Mexico Territory, that he had died bravely. Everything was in tumult,

Mama said, Federal forces moving out, Confederates coming in. Papa had always been a Union man, so Mama moved to Grayson County, in North Texas, to live with her brother and sister-in-law. Her brother, Ephraim Grelle, he was a Union man, too, and there were a lot of Unionists in that part of the state.

That's where I was born.

Trouble came there, too. Trouble came everywhere in those terrible years. I must have just turned one year old when a bunch of screaming men from the militia stormed into Uncle Ephraim and Aunt Matilda's house one night. They arrested Uncle Ephraim. Arrested I don't know how many Union men all over the county, all over North Texas. And then, later, they hanged them. Hanged forty of them, more than forty, maybe as many as fifty, I don't know. They hanged Uncle Ephraim. Strung them all up on an elm tree in Gainesville after some kind of trial. Well, the Rebels called it a trial. Mama always called it murder. And later, when Little Ephraim ran off . . . he was maybe fifteen, sixteen, I guess . . . the Rebels hanged Aunt Matilda, said Little Ephraim was a draft dodger and that they'd hang him, too, if ever they caught him. Said he wasn't no better than his Yankee-loving pa, and they'd hang the whole lot of us, me included.

So Mama ran off, crying, shattered, made it to Dallas, she said, and then found someone who carried her . . . us, I mean . . . down to the Hill Country. Fredericksburg. We didn't know anybody in town, but there were Union people there, and the Texas Rebs didn't hound them as much. Didn't hang them anyway.

Like I said, I was too young at the time to remember any of what happened in Gainesville, or much of anything during the rest of the war. But I do remember Mama, remember her telling me how they didn't even bury Uncle Ephraim proper, how the hogs rooted out the graves. I remember her sobbing most nights, worrying so that my father had had at least a decent burial. He was a brave man, a good man, would have been a good father. She wanted to know that he was resting in peace, wanted a marble tombstone over his grave, wanted him remembered for posterity, didn't want him to wind up like Uncle Ephraim and those Rebel hogs.

Mama . . . she . . . she died . . . in July. Don't feel sorry. It was a blessing, I think. I know it was. A blessing. In many ways she had died when Papa was killed, or at least after all that happened in North Texas back in the autumn of 'Sixty-Two. She was a seamstress, lived in Fredericksburg the rest of her life, never made much money, but she saw to it that I got an education, saw to it that I read the Good Book, saw to it that I remembered my father even if he had died before I came into this world. I was with her when she was called to Glory, holding her hand, telling her that everything would be all right.

And the last thing Mama said to me, she said, was . . . "See to your Papa, Eleora."

I owed Mama that much. I owed Papa. If Mama had any money, if she hadn't been so devastated by Papa's death and then that . . . that . . . that nightmare she lived through . . . lived through trying to keep me safe, from evil's clutches, mind you . . . in Grayson County and Gainesville, or struggling to keep me fed and a roof over my head all those years . . . why, I remember seeing her fingers bleed, remember her soaking her hands, sore, so sore, from all her hard work. Well, if she had been up to it, hadn't been saddled with me, I warrant she would have headed West to locate Papa. But she couldn't.

So I did. Well, tried. . . .

After we buried Mama, after I settled all her affairs, I took what little money we had saved and went to San Antonio, started trying to find out what I could about Papa. It took a few months, took a lot of scouting, reading old newspapers, hunting up old-timers, but I did it. Some old Overland men knew about John James Giddings, sent me to El Paso, then Mesilla, finally Lordsburg. That's where I met. . . .

Oh, I can't bear to think about what happened to that poor, poor man.

Thanks, honey. I'll be all right. Coffee's strong. Hot. First hot coffee I've had since I can't remember when. I've been too scared to light a fire, just that candle every now and then when I'd get real scared. Well . . . well . . . anyway, Mister Spoon said he remembered all about Papa. He didn't know him, never met him, but he knew about that stagecoach the Apaches had hit in April of 'Sixty-One. Twenty years ago. He was freighting supplies to Fort Breckinridge, coming toward Doubtful Cañon, when they discovered the ruins of what once had been a stagecoach station. They found a man there, odd-looking bird, Mister Spoon recalled, who said he had been on the stage heading to California with Mister Giddings. They had arrived, the man had told Mister Spoon, after the attack on the station, found the well poisoned, had buried the men killed by the Indians, then went on. Mister Giddings had to get through, the man had said. But. . . .

But . . . he didn't. Poor Papa.

Mister Spoon said they found the stagecoach down in the cañon, found the dead men, buried them. He said my father had died bravely, but I knew that already, knew it from Mama's stories, but, yeah, it sure felt good to hear it from someone who had been there, well, maybe not there at the time, but someone who had at least seen the aftermath, had read the sign. Mister Spoon, he said he could read sign as good as any Army scout.

He told me he'd be glad to take me to Papa's grave, that he knew exactly where it was. All I wanted was to see it, to make sure it would satisfy Mama, then maybe come back with a handsome stone. I remember one time asking Mama, before she took sick real bad, if she wanted to be laid to rest alongside Papa. Not in New Mexico, but we could bring his remains to a real cemetery in a real churchyard, but she had told me, no, that she'd be with Papa soon enough, together in heaven, and that it would mean more for Papa to lie near where he had so bravely fallen, as long as his grave was good and he had a monument and Christian blessing.

Well, Mister Spoon and I rode out, on horses and with a pack mule, and he was such a gentleman. He warned me of the dangers in the cañon, as had everyone in Lordsburg and Mesilla, but I just had to see it. I saw it.

Briefly.

Then I heard the screams.

Mister Spoon pushed me aside, shoved a rifle into my hands, told me to run, and not look back, and I ran. I ran and ran and ran, and I heard the shots, the screams. I was terrified. I don't remember what all happened, I just remember running. See my clothes? Scratches? The Apaches didn't do this. I did all that myself. Tore up my clothes in yucca and catclaw. I hid. I think I did. Found a little cave, well, not even a cave, just, well, a hole or something, and I hid there after all the screaming, all the gunshots, after everything had grown quiet. I heard men walking, ever so softly, heard them talking in some strange voice. I even saw two of them, and knew for certain that they would see me, but they didn't. They were just kids. Boys. Not much older than you children. And then they walked off, and, when it grew dark, when the moon came out, I just walked back here. I've been here since, waiting, praying.

I'm sorry I shot at you. Sorry I didn't believe you, but I've been here for days, hiding. Mister Spoon told me that I shouldn't trust anyone we'd meet in Doubtful Cañon. For all I knew, you were outlaws. I'm sorry. I . . . I just want to go home.

After leaning his Winchester against the wall near the door, Whitey Grey came back to Eleora Giddings and took the cup from her hand, walked to the hearth, and refilled it with coffee. Then he drank, considering her story, or maybe our plight.

With Jasmine and Ian Spencer Henry tending and comforting Miss Giddings, I went to the albino.

"You should tell her," I told him.

"Tell her what?"

"About her father. You knew him. You saw him die. I think it would comfort her."

"I don't want to," he said petulantly.

"I don't mean tell her how he died. She's upset enough, has been through enough. But you knew him. You should tell her."

"Don't want to," he repeated.

I tried a different subject. "Should I stand guard? In case the Apaches hit us?"

"They ain't," he said. "Iffen they was, they'd done

it by now. Woman's right. Said it was nothin' but boys. That's all I seen when they attacked us. Boys. Twelve, fourteen, no older than fifteen, I warrant. Boys from San Carlos wantin' to prove they's good ol' Apaches. Show off for that Geronimo and all 'em other big bucks that took flight."

"Boys?" Well, I recalled, it certainly had been a young lad trying to cut my throat back in the cañon.

"Don't get careless, Jack, just 'cause they ain't much older'n you. You's seen how tough 'em Cherry Cows is even when they ain't full growed." The white-skinned man warmed up his cup with another splash of bitter brew. "Baby rattler's just as deadly as a big one."

Then shouldn't someone stand guard? I wondered, but held my tongue on that subject, instead asking: "Well, what are we going to do with Miss Giddings?"

"Gots to study on it."

"I still think you should tell her. . . ."

"Boy, I ramrod this outfit. And I's gettin' sick and tired of remindin' you that."

He took another drink of coffee, only to spray into my face when Ian Spencer Henry asked Eleora Giddings: "What about the gold?"

"Shut up, boy!" he thundered, shoving me aside, while I was frantically wiping my eyes and nose, brushing the coffee away. By the time I had recovered, Whitey Grey stood over a cowering Ian Spencer Henry, raising his fist in an intimidating gesture.

"What gold?" Eleora Giddings asked.

The albino cursed and groaned.

"Mister Grey was there," Ian Spencer Henry said. "He was with your father. He's the one Willie Spoon found at the old station. That 'odd-looking' one. We're here. . . ."

Another oath. Whitey Grey let out a howl and marched back to the door, picking up the Winchester, staring into the morning.

"You . . . you were there?" Miss Giddings asked.

"Don't pay 'em chil'ren no never mind," he said, shifting the rifle.

"He was there, all right," Ian Spencer Henry informed her. "You should hear his story. It's all blood and thunder and glory. Tell her, Mister Grey. Tell her all about it. Tell her about her daddy. Tell her about the gold!"

"What gold?" she asked again.

And, again, Whitey Grey cursed.

Eventually, though, he handed me the Winchester, told me to keep an eye out, and walked back to Eleora Giddings. "Name's Grey," he said. "Folks call me Whitey. On account of . . . well, I reckon you can see plain enough. I rode for the Overland. And I was a gun hand, messenger, guard, conductor, whatever you want to call it, when Mister Giddings, your pa, took off from Texas to Californy on that fateful ride."

Squatting, his fingers working nervously, he told her the story, pretty much the same tale he had regaled us with back at the Lady Macbeth Mine, although he skipped some of the blood, toned down much of the thunder, and added theatrics and heroics to the death of her father, which he kept brief. "Bravest man I ever knowed," he said, "your pappy was." He also failed to mention the $30,000. When he had finished, he pulled the severed Apache ear from his pocket and tossed out one final embellishment.

"Here, I kilt me one Cherry Cow that I knowed had a hand in your pappy's death." He glared at Ian

Spencer Henry to keep silent, and I guess his fib was in the right place, disgusting as it was. "You can have it iffen you wants," he told Miss Giddings.

"No . . . thanks."

The ear returned to Whitey Grey's pocket. " 'Tain't nothin' much," he said.

"What about the gold?" she asked.

The glare fell on Ian Spencer Henry again, but this time Whitey Grey sighed heavily, sank onto the dirt floor, and spit out the truth. "Your pappy was in charge of gettin' thirty thousand dollars in gold out of Texas and into bluebelly territory in Californy. When the Apaches hit us, when it was plumb certain we'd all get rubbed out, he went to bury 'em saddlebags, make sure 'em Cherry Cows didn't get that money. Well, he did just that. Died brave and game doin' it."

"How did you make it out alive?" she asked.

"Same as you," he answered. "Pure luck. Injuns never been much good at finishin' a fight. Reckon they gots bored."

"We're going to get the gold," Ian Spencer Henry said.

The white-skinned man, looking a little flushed, ground his teeth. The petrified woman, looking a little confused, stared at Jasmine.

"And?" Eleora Giddings asked.

Jasmine shrugged.

"Dig it up," Ian Spencer Henry said. "Hey, I got a great idea. Mister Grey said he'd give us five thousand dollars to help find the treasure. That's why we're here."

"I. . . ." Miss Giddings shook her head. "I don't know. I guess I thought he was your grandfather."

"No." Ian Spencer Henry cackled. "No, he ain't

nothing like that. We'd never seen him till he scared us almost to death back in Shakespeare. No, what I was saying is this . . . we're not greedy. You can have a share of our five thousand dollars. The math's easier that way. Four instead of dividing by three."

Now Whitey Grey perked up, liking and approving Ian Spencer Henry's plan.

"That's one thousand two hundred and fifty dollars. For each of us. That would buy you a mighty big marble cross to put over your pa's grave, don't you think?" When Eleora Giddings didn't respond, Ian Spencer Henry, as was his nature, kept right on talking. "Me? I thought I'd have sixteen hundred dollars and then some, but I can make a good fortune with twelve hundred fifty. Do you know how many half-dime novels that'll buy? Twenty-five thousand. And if I sell them for seven cents in Shakespeare? That's . . . let's see . . . that's. . . . That's seventeen hundred and fifty dollars. Five hundred dollars profit. That's something." He grinned and concluded with a brag. "I done all that in my head."

"That's something," Miss Giddings said. She studied Whitey Grey. "But that money . . . if it's still there . . . don't you think that belongs to . . . ?"

"John Butterfield's dead," the albino cut her off. "Been dead a long time. Your pa and everyone on that stagecoach is dead, 'ceptin' me. There ain't no Overland company no more, and Wells, Fargo and Company ain't gots no claim on that gold. Nobody else does, neither, but one. I figure that's me. Figure I deserves it, and the boy's makin' good sense. You deserve it, too. Some of it, I mean. Iffen you wants to, I'm willin' to take you on with my other pards."

"Pards?" She looked skeptical. "Why on earth did you bring these children here?"

"They come of their own accord."

Well, that wasn't entirely true.

She started to say something, probably a protest, but Whitey Grey started again. "You ain't gots to come with us. You can wait here by your lonesome, hope 'em Apaches don't come back, hope no contrary bandit decides to spend the night here. I ain't hankerin' to stay in that cañon any longer than I gots to. The chil'ren and me gots us two centipede cars hobbled over at the S.P. tracks near Stein's Peak. We get the gold, today, and get out of here . . . today, tomorrow at the latest. Light a shuck back to Lordsburg. That's. . . ."

He never finished. Whitey Grey had a keen sense of hearing, detecting the horses before I heard the *clattering* of hoofs. A moment later, I spied a figure galloping along the road, reining up in a hurry and staring at the house. He was dressed like a cowhand, striped britches shoved inside tall boots, clad in a linen duster over a bib-front shirt, a black Stetson pulled low on his head, mounted on a tall sorrel horse while pulling a saddled buckskin behind him. I couldn't make out his face, but could tell he wore a gun belt, although he kept his hands away from the holstered revolver or the rifle in the saddle scabbard.

Whitey Grey slammed shut the door, barred it—something Miss Giddings had forgotten to do—and jerked the Winchester from my hands, then, crouching, moved to the open window.

"Tarnation!" he said. "I knowed we shouldn't have lit that fire. That *hombre*'s smelt our smoke, knows we're here. Wants my gold, I warrant, but I gots too many pards already. Well, I's gonna fix his flint."

"He's not an Apache," I said. My eyes widened in

horror as the albino brought up the Winchester and took aim at the mounted figure who kept calling out a loud, and friendly: "Halloooo!"

"No, sir, he ain't," Whitey Grey whispered, and grinned. "But they's all kinds of snakes in Doubtful Cañon."

Chapter Fourteen

"You should know, Whitey," came a cottony voice from the rear window.

Everyone but Whitey Grey whirled to see a handsome man leaning inside the back window, a deadly Remington revolver pointed at the albino's back. Grey had too much experience to spin. He just muttered an oath, and took his finger off the Winchester's trigger.

"Put the rifle down, Whitey," the man said. "Or I'll put you down."

With another curse, Whitey Grey let the Winchester topple out the window. Slowly, raising his hands slightly, he faced the gunman.

I knew this dark-haired man, but couldn't place him until he climbed through the window, lithe as a cat. "It's all right!" he yelled to the man on horseback. "And the coffee's on!"

He wore a black hat, red shirt, and canvas jacket, sporting two holsters on a shell belt around his slim waist, and gray trousers tucked inside tan boots with mule-ear pulls flapping on the sides. *The boots.* I'd seen him trying them on back at Mr. Shankin's store in Shakespeare.

"Comfortable," a second voice said a short while

later, and I studied the other man, now standing in the door. He swept off his Stetson when he saw Eleora Giddings.

" 'Morning, ma'am. I'm. . . ."

"Curly Bill Brocious," I said.

The man by the window laughed. "You're famous, Billy."

"It's good to be that way." Brocious pulled the hat back over his dark locks. "Sometimes. Yes, ma'am, the kid's right. I'm William Brocious, but my friends call me Curly Bill. Over yonder's my friend. We call him Dutch, but his name's Johnny Ringo."

Brocious picked up the old Henry repeater, studied the bullet-splintered stock, and pitched it out the open door.

After shoving the Remington into the empty holster on his left hip, Dutch Ringo tipped his hat. "John Peters Ringo. Didn't mean to give y'all a fright," he said. "But didn't want to get shot dead, either."

"Especially since we're friendly folks," Brocious added. "Coffee sure smells inviting."

"Only gots one cup." Shuffling his feet, eyes darting, Whitey Grey mumbled his words.

"No biscuits?" Ringo said. "No bacon or slumgullion or fried quail eggs?"

"We haven't had anything to eat in a 'coon's age," Jasmine said.

"Well, that's not healthy," Ringo said. "Not healthy at all. Kids and, likewise, grown-ups need to eat. Curly, put our horses in the corral, bring in our saddlebags. We'll have us a veritable feast. But I'd feel more comfortable if you . . ."—he jutted his jaw toward the albino—"would kindly toss your Colt outside. Slowly, Whitey. Very slowly."

"You want my gun, too?" Ian Spencer Henry asked.

"Huh?"

"My gun? Do you want it, too? It's my Pa's, though, so I'd like it back. He'll whup me good if I lose it." Ian Spencer Henry fished out the old Army Colt, which prompted a short chuckle from both gunmen.

"That's all right, son," Ringo said. "You keep it. Might have need of it if we run into bandits."

"Or Earps," Brocious said with a laugh, and walked outside.

Famished, we ate heartily, greedily, devouring fried bacon, cold tortillas, and posole, and a fresh pot of coffee that Dutch Ringo made more to his liking. Brocious even passed out peppermint candy sticks to the three children. It was a feast. After we ate, stretching out on the hard floor, enjoying our candy while Brocious fetched knife and tobacco plug from his pocket and leaned against the door frame, keeping, as Ringo had suggested, one eye on the cañon road and the other on Whitey Grey.

"So," Ringo said, nodding at the pale man. "You finally decided to dig up that gold."

"You been trailin' me, Ringy?" the albino asked.

"Not at all. I hadn't given you a minute's reflection since Arkansas, Mister Grey. Not until Curly and I overheard this boy." His head tilted at me. "Back in Shakespeare."

My eyes tried to avoid the albino's murderous glare, and, when I worked up enough courage to look at my two friends, their angry faces said I had betrayed them as well. "I . . . I didn't know," I said.

"It's not his fault," Ringo said. "Curly and I were

on our way to Tombstone, but, well, Curly wore out his welcome last year after a little accident involving the marshal there. And, oh, we reckon that money you claim is still in the cañon is more tempting than trying to buck the tiger or finding some beef for the Clantons to sell."

"Twenty years," Brocious said, failing to stifle a burp. "What makes you dead certain it's still there?"

Whitey Grey didn't answer until Brocious aimed the Winchester at his abdomen.

"Man has to know where to look," the albino said. "Then he has to be able to gets it. I reckon it's still there."

"So." Ringo tipped his head back. "The lady comes to see her daddy's grave. You come for the gold. Curly and I decide to place our bets on you. But why three shirt-tail kids?"

"They's my pards," Whitey Grey said. "This lady's my pard. You ain't my pard, Ringy. You neither, Brocious."

"We are now," Brocious said. "We shared our grub with you. That cuts us in."

Leave it to Ian Spencer Henry to interrupt the conversation, and at least ease some tension. "Jasmine, Jack, and Miss Giddings and me are splitting five thousand dollars," he said. "You want some of that?"

Brocious chortled, and Ringo grinned. "How much gold did you say there was, Grey?"

"I didn't."

"Thirty thousand," Ian Spencer Henry interjected.

"That's what I thought. Well, I think Curly and I deserve more than five thousand."

"You might not get anything, but your own tombstone," Miss Giddings said, her voice tight, but forceful. She didn't care one whit for Curly Bill Brocious or Dutch Ringo, and I couldn't blame her. Whitey Grey was one thing. Not that we trusted him, not that he wasn't cold-blooded, but Ringo and Brocious made my skin crawl. I truly believe, well, most times anyway, that if we did find that treasure, Whitey Grey would give us $5,000. But men like Curly Bill Brocious and Johnny Ringo? They would slit our throats without compunction.

"Apaches killed Mister Spoon, a kindly gentleman who had guided me to my father's grave," Miss Giddings said. "Apaches almost killed me. And they attacked Mister Grey and these children yesterday evening. For all I know, those Indians are still there. Or maybe surrounding us, waiting for their chance."

The two gunmen shot each other a quick stare, and then both men shrugged.

"Life's like faro. It's a gamble." Ringo pulled a bottle of amber fluid out of the saddlebag. He withdrew the cork, took a swig, and tossed the whiskey to Brocious. Whitey Grey wet his lips, but said nothing.

"How do you know him?" I asked Ringo, pointing at the albino.

"Maybe they met in Detroit," Ian Spencer Henry offered. "Mister Grey's been in all the big cities. And my ma. . . ." He didn't finish.

Laughing so hard, Ringo almost fumbled the bottle Brocious pitched back to him. Once he had recovered and had another drink, he laughed again, wiped his mouth with his jacket sleeve, and shook his head. "Yeah, I bet he has. I first met him in a *cantina* in Mason County, Texas, some years back. He had just gotten out of prison in Huntsville. When was that, Whitey? 'Seventy-One, right? I was celebrating my twenty-first birthday if I recollect correctly. Rustling, wasn't it?"

"In the Yuma jail," Brocious added, "I think it was assault. Who sent you to Detroit? Judge Parker?"

"A misunderstandin'," the albino muttered. "Demon rum."

"Uhn-huh." Ringo took another pull from the bottle and passed it back to Brocious. "Selling rum in the Choctaw Nation, and then busting a bottle over a federal deputy's face. That'll earn you some hard time in the Detroit House of Corrections. I was having a drink in a Van Buren parlor house when they arrested him. That's the last time we ran into each other. Five years ago. That's about right."

Ian Spencer Henry scratched his head. "Prison? You mean he's been in prison?"

"Just about every prison or jail known to man," Ringo said. "In Texas and Arkansas, I never believed those stories you were telling when in your cups, Grey, but now I'm not so sure. I always thought you were just mad."

"He gets mad," Ian Spencer Henry said. "He gets mad a lot."

"That's not my meaning," Ringo said.

My friend pondered this a moment, his eyes darting from Whitey Grey to Dutch Ringo. At last he said: "Oh."

Ringo caught the bottle again, took a final swallow, returned the cork, and shoved the whiskey back into the leather bag. "Here's the deal, folks. I'm going to listen to Whitey Grey's story again. All of us will. If Curly and I decide this story might be true, we'll join up with you. And we like the split. Five thousand for you. The rest for Curly and me."

"And the Apaches?" Brocious asked.

"The Apaches don't get a split." Ringo laughed at his own joke, shook his head, and told his partner: "My bet's that those Indians have already lit a shuck. Army patrols are all over chasing those that jumped San Carlos."

"They've hit the cañon twice," Brocious warned.

"You can back out, Curly," Ringo said bitterly, his mood turning savage. Dismissing Brocious, Ringo drew a revolver, a Thunderer this time, aiming it at the white-skinned man. "If Curly and I figure that, yeah, you're just some old reprobate touched in your head, then we'll leave you be. You can dig for gold, dig for water, or dig your own grave. I don't care. But, first, Whitey, I want to hear that story."

"You've heard it, Ringy," the albino said. "Eavesdropped on us a little while ago."

The gunman nodded. "Yeah. I heard you tell the lady here. Heard you tell it in Mason. And in Van Buren. Curly heard it in Yuma. But this time. . . ." He rested the revolver on his knee, sighted down the barrel. "This time . . . I want to hear the truth."

When Grey folded his arms across his chest, Ringo thumbed back the hammer on the double-action .41. "I'd be doing the lady and the kids a favor by killing you, Grey," he said icily.

With a heavy sigh, the albino sank to his knees, shaking his head. "Happened just like I tol' y'all," he said.

"The truth, you ivory-faced cretin," Brocious snapped. "Dutch here'll know if you're lying to us. Dutch always knows a liar."

The albino muttered an oath, sat back, and shook

his head. "Mostly," he said. "Happened 'most like I said it afore."

Reluctantly he started again.

We left the station at Franklin. Mister Giddings, old Sam Golden, and me. I volunteered. Was the only hand with enough sand to make the trip across New Mexico, what with Cochise and his bucks on the prod. Mister Giddings, he didn't like that. Not a bit. Didn't like me. Didn't trust me, and he tol' 'em fellers at the Texas Division how he druther ride with the devil than with ol' Whitey Grey as his guard. But he didn't have no choice. The Overland was all but belly-up, Rebs was movin' through Texas, bluecoat Army was lightin' out of Texas. He was stuck with me. 'Sides, he did know I was right handy with a six-shooter or rifle. Knowed I could handle myself in a fight.

Yeah, I wanted that gold. Wanted it for my own-self. Thirty thousand dollars? In gold coin? That was temptin'. And it was a long way from Texas to Califorry. Mister Giddings knowed that. He wouldn't let 'em saddlebags, heavy as they was, out of his sight. I couldn't touch 'em. Nobody could, 'ceptin' him. And once we come to Mesilla, he up and hired him two other shootists. The Mex and Bruce from Wisconsin. Tol' Bruce to keep his eyes peeled for Apaches and secesh, but never to take his eyes offen me, neither.

Like I done said afore, we didn't see much of nothin' betwixt Mesilla and Stein's Peak station, and then we seen all that death. Apaches had killed ever' last soul at the station, run off the stock, put poison in the well. And it happened just like I tol' this here lady, tol' these chil'ren. "My word," Mister Giddings, he says when he's seein' all 'em dead folk, and I tells him . . . "Ain't no word for it." And then I tells him . . . "Smart thing, Mister Giddings, might be to turn back."

See, I wanted to turn back. Gold or no gold, I didn't fancy gettin' myself kilt by no Apaches, and, well, maybe he'd just give up the fight, go back to Texas, see things the way they should be seen. Maybe Mister Giddings would decide that money'd be better suited for him. He said his wife was in the family way. Thought that might change the tune he was singin', once he thunk on it some. I figgered I might be able to talk some sense into him, but, no, he was one hard-rock customer. He had his orders, he says, says he ain't turnin' back. Says we ain't turnin' back. Like I say, Mister Giddings had a belly full of gumption.

So we went on. Through the cañon here, and down yonder. Right where we buried Willie Spoon.

That fight happened, too, just like I tol' it afore. Mostly, anyhows. The Apaches hit us right when we was in the cañon. Shot the Mex and Sam Golden off the box, and I climbed up to get the reins, Apaches yippin' and shootin'. Air filled with arrows and lead and dust. You seen the cañon. You know how narrow it is. Well, we wrecked. Busted ourselves up pretty good. Bruce got kilt just like I said. And Mister Giddings, he knowed it was hopeless. Knowed we was all done for.

I tells him it wasn't no such thing. Said we'd get out of here, but maybe I should bury that gold. And he laughed at me. He drawed his pistol, said he'd see me dead afore he ever let me touch the gold. And he run. I started after him, but got into a li'l' tussle with a Cherry Cow buck. Then I hoofed it to the cañon wall, hobbled as fast as I could, my leg hurt like it was. I'm lookin' for Mister Giddings, and he comes slidin' down a little mound, an arrow in his shoulder, his leg bleedin' somethin' fierce. He tells me he's buried the gold.

"The Apaches shall not have it, Mister Grey," he says. "And nor shall you, you treacherous piece of filth."

That's what he says to me. Well, I stare up that hill, and 'neath this juniper I see just a sliver in the rock. Li'l cave it is. He's dropped the bags in there. I ain't no big man, but 'tain't no way I can gets in that hole.

"It's deep, too." Mr. Giddings, he's laughing at me. Reckon he was plumb out of his mind.

Don't matter none. I couldn't get up that hill, not with a horde of Cherry Cows after us, and, even if I did, I couldn't wriggle down in that li'l' hole in the cañon. Now, it's gettin' nigh dark, and I knowed if I can just hold out that long, well, maybe . . . just maybe. . . . But the Apaches is comin' with a mind to finish the fight before the sun goes down, and Mister Giddings, he's just laughin'. Mad he was. But he wasn't payin' no attention to me, howlin', and I taken my revolver and knocked that pistol out of his hands. Had a mind to kill him, I did, him treatin' me like dirt, him takin' my money from me like he done. Only here come the Apaches. Then it strikes me what to do. I shoved Mister Giddings out there, into the open. And while 'em bucks are carvin' him up, havin' some fun, tearin' him to pieces, I hightail it back up the cañon.

The Apaches sent two braves after me. I fetched one to perdition. Wounded the other. And then hid in the rocks till it come full night. Then I sneaked my way back to the station. Waited Reckon I was 'bout out of my head, too. Then Willie Spoon and 'em freighters come. I joins up with 'em, and we bury the dead. Bury Mister Giddings. His bones anyway.

Now, all this time durin' the buryin', I'm lookin' for that hole, that juniper, but, well, wasn't nothin' I could do then. Didn't have no horse. And there must've been practically twenty men hired on with that train. Wasn't of a mind to share that gold with 'em. Not that many of 'em, and couldn't trust 'em. And, yeah, there were those Apaches to think 'bout. So it struck me that that gold wasn't goin' nowhere, and I just grinned like a fool. John Butterfield, he'd think either the Apaches gots it or it gots buried and the location died with Mister Giddings. That's what I let 'em Overland boys in Tucson believe.

Figgered I'd come back for it when the Apaches was gone, or at least not so troublesome. Would have come back sooner, maybe, but, well, there was all 'em misunderstandin's between me and 'em lawdogs here and there.

That's how it was. And that's the gospel.

Chapter Fifteen

When Whitey Grey finished his story, Miss Eleora Giddings slapped his face, a savage hit that sounded like a cannon round in the rock house.

"You . . . !" Trembling with rage, she struck him again, knocking off his hat, and the white-skinned man accepted his punishment. "You murdered my father!"

"Apaches done it," he said softly.

Another wallop.

" 'Twas him or me, and he was bad off. Cherry Cows would've kilt both of us. Almost done it anyhow."

This time she balled both fists and punched his head, let out a terrible groan, stepped back, shaking her stung hands, and sank to her knees. She started to sob, but quickly choked it off, and took a deep breath. She cursed Whitey Grey.

Curly Bill Brocious just laughed. His partner appeared to be deep in contemplation, pondering the albino's story, showing no concern for the upset young woman. He smoothed his mustache and, his mood now amiable, asked Brocious to share his thoughts.

The gunman took a final glance outside and, turn-

ing to face Ringo, shrugged. "Ain't seen hide nor hair
of no Apaches. Cañon looks deserted."

"Last night's storm likely took the fight out of
them," Ringo offered.

"Could be." Brocious pointed at Whitey Grey.
"You believe his yarn?"

"It adds up. You?"

Another shrug. "I've bet on worse hands. But I
don't get why the kids are here."

"I do." Dutch Ringo grinned when the albino and
the children looked at him. I had wondered that
myself, had toyed with various theories but never
really liked anything I had considered.

"The freak says that hole in the cañon was too
small for him. He hasn't shrunk any in twenty years,
so he figures a child can wriggle into that pit, get
those saddlebags. You kidnap them, Grey?"

The albino snorted, wet his lips, rough fingers
tracing the blotches on his cheeks left by Miss Giddings's hits. His eyes avoided Ian Spencer Henry,
Jasmine, and me, and he shuffled his feet and muttered: "Tol' me they was orphans. But they lied."

"Runaways?" Brocious shook his head. "I don't
know about this now, Dutch. Their parents . . . maybe
the sheriff . . . they'll be combing this territory for
those young 'uns."

"Is that true?" Ringo asked Ian Spencer Henry,
who naturally told him everything: how many days
we'd been gone from Shakespeare, our adventures
along the Southern Pacific tracks and through *Valle
de las Playas*, and, how his father would barely notice
he was even missing, that Jasmine's dad had been
killed (he left out the particulars), and that my father had been in an accident that had left his two
legs broken.

Where Ian Spencer Henry came up with that lie, I don't know, but I understood why he had chosen to tell such a stretcher. Out of respect for me. He didn't want those outlaws to know my father was a drunkard. They could think what they wanted of his own addle-brained father, but Ian Spencer Henry would protect Jasmine Allison and me. His goodwill and loyalty ran deep. We couldn't have asked for a better partner, or friend.

"I like this here boy, Dutch," Brocious said. "He can ride with me anytime."

"I like the girl better." Ringo nodded at Jasmine. "She doesn't say a word."

Brocious shook his head. "Dumb fool girls," he said, his eyes moving from Jasmine to Miss Giddings. "None of them should ever have left home. This country ain't for the gentler sex. Respectable women, I mean."

"I'm all for riding with you, Curly Bill," Ian Spencer Henry sang out. "We could be famous, get written up by Mister Buntline or Colonel Ingraham. Those are two of my favorite authors. And I figure I've got the right name to be a great scout or trapper or bad guy. Two of my names are the same as fast-shooting rifles."

Brocious ran his fingers through my friend's hair. "That so. Sakes alive, though, I never heard of an Ian rifle. How's it compare to the Winchester?"

"Nooooo." Ian Spencer Henry started to correct Brocious, not catching the gunman's joke, but Ringo cut him off.

"You still haven't given me reason to believe the good citizens of Shakespeare haven't formed a posse and are tracking you down." His head tilted at me. "There's no law in Shakespeare, but I know this boy has friends in town. The skinflint at the mercantile seemed to favor the lad when we were getting outfitted. And I don't want to be mistaken for some child stealer, get caught between an angry, worried father and his kid."

"You won't," my friend assured him. "Besides, Jack here left a letter in the Lady Macbeth Mine to throw any searchers off the trail, someone like Mister Shankin, I reckon. When they find it and read it, they'll think we've run off to El Paso. So that's where they'll be looking, if they ever get around to looking. East of Shakespeare. Not west. Not here."

Upon hearing of this chicanery, Ringo gave me a moment's consideration. "Smart lad," he said. "The boys and me can always use a good liar. Look me up when you grow up a few more inches, say in about two or three years."

"In two or three years," I said, "you'll likely be dead." His face dropped, and Curly Bill Brocious let out a loud howl, but I spun to the killer and told him: "You, too, Curly." He kept on laughing, even when I said: "Maybe in two or three more hours."

"By you?" Brocious asked, snorting and bellowing, dabbing his watering eyes with the ends of his bandanna.

"Apaches," I said. "I'm not sure they're gone."

Brooding, Dutch Ringo withdrew his whiskey bottle again, his eyes malevolent, and I felt relieved Curly Bill Brocious found some humor in my remarks. If not, Ringo might have shot me. I'm not sure why I said it, or even if I really thought the Apaches might be lying in wait for us, ready to wipe us out, for what Ringo said had made sense. In all likelihood, the savage storm of the previous night had driven the Indians away.

"You could be right, kid," Brocious said. With a final snigger, he walked over to Ringo, helped himself to a drink, corked the bottle, and told his partner, his words evenly spaced and tough: "Braced yourself enough for the day's work, Dutch. I'd like you sober. Kid could be right. Apaches, the law, Mexican bandits, or the Army. Anything could be waiting for us in that cañon."

"All right." Ringo's voice was just above a whisper. My words, somehow, had unnerved him. That I found strange. A man like Dutch Johnny Ringo had no fear.

Brocious walked over to the albino. "But why three kids, Grey? I still don't quite savvy that."

Our former leader looked slightly embarrassed. "Wasn't sure they'd all come," he said.

"Story! He's telling a story!" Ian Spencer Henry said. "He said we all had to come with him. That it was all of us or none of us. Said he'd kill any of us that turned back on him. You're supposed to tell the truth, Mister Grey. Dutch Ringo will know if you're fibbing or not."

"That is the truth," the white-skinned man said. "Yeah, I threatened 'em. Tried to scare 'em. But I didn't think they'd all come. But they did."

"And you're glad of it," Ringo said. "Isn't that right?"

After a long wait, the albino's head bobbed.

"Tell them why, you miserable mistake of nature."

When no answer came, Ringo, his despondency having faded, laughed. "He just needs one kid," he told me, and I knew he meant that as a threat. The man had a vindictive streak wider than a quarter-section. "This is tough country. One of you kids might have gotten killed. Might still get killed. That ivory-faced fool, he was just playing the odds." He laughed again, a cold, callow laugh. "What do you say, Curly? Should we kill two of these children now? Be less trouble."

Brocious's eyes widened. Finally he smiled, but I doubted if he knew for certain if Ringo were serious or not. "Still might have need, Dutch. Like you said, this is dangersome country. It would be a shame if we didn't have no kid to volunteer to climb into that hole." He tilted his head toward the albino. "But what about him?"

"We need him," Ringo said. "For now. He'll point us to the spot. What did you say, freak? About two miles into the cañon?"

No answer came, and the outlaws didn't press the matter. "Doesn't matter," Ringo said. "It's near this lady's daddy's grave. Let's go find it."

"What about her?" Brocious pointed at Miss Giddings.

"Bring her along, too," Ringo said with a crooked grin. "After all, we're all partners."

For the second time in my life, for the second time in as many days, I began the descent into Doubtful Cañon.

Whitey Grey led the way on foot, his head down, thumbs hooked in his britches, downcast, knowing he had lost, had lost after twenty years of dreaming. I almost felt sorry for him.

Miss Giddings walked along with Ian Spencer Henry, Jasmine, and me, about fifteen yards behind the albino, Ian Spencer Henry protecting us, or so he said, pointing the .44 Colt toward one side of the cañon, then the other. He had given me his sling-shot, which I stuck in my back pocket. Twenty yards behind us rode Curly Bill Brocious, keeping along the left side of the cañon, as close to the wall as his horse would let him. On the opposite side rode Dutch Johnny Ringo.

Rain had cleansed the ground, purified the cañon, it struck me, and the air smelled sweet, the *clopping* of the hoofs behind us in dark contrast to the desert landscape's raw beauty.

"Do you really believe what you said?"

Her voice surprised me, for Miss Giddings had said nothing since attacking Whitey Grey back in the rock house. I looked up, never slacking my pace, and saw her staring at Ian Spencer Henry, who lowered his gun.

"Ma'am?"

"What you said about your parents? Your father?"

He frowned, looked away. "My pa don't care a thing about me. My ma, neither. She run off to Ann Arbor, left me. Me and Pa both. My pa don't know I'm alive, just like he never noticed my ma."

His voice choked at the last few words, and tears glistened in my own eyes. I'd never really understood that about my friend. I never knew how much he hurt, perhaps because all of that time I had been so preoccupied with my own pain.

"And, you, child?" she asked me. "Did your father really break both of his legs in a mining accident?"

Refusing to let the tears come, I answered her coldly. "No, ma'am. He's a drunk. He's been a walking whiskey keg ever since. . . ." I couldn't hold back the tears, cursed as they streamed down my face, attacking them, sniffling, making myself stop crying. I made myself finish. "Ever since my mother and sisters died. Diphtheria."

"I'm sorry," she said softly. "But you still have your father."

"No, I don't!" I shouted, surprised to hear my words echoing across the cañon.

"Shut up!" Ringo barked. "Don't let half the territory know where we are."

I waited until we had traveled twenty more yards. "I don't have my father. Whiskey's got him."

I kicked a stone savagely. I wanted to run away, to catch up with Whitey Grey, walk with him, or maybe just keep running until Dutch Ringo shot me in the back. Yet I couldn't. Staring ahead, I walked, fighting back the tears as they tried to blind me, tried to block out anything Miss Giddings said. Trying to, but failing.

"How about you . . . Jasmine, isn't it?"

Jasmine Allison wet her lips. "That's right," was all she said.

"Your father. He is dead, isn't he?"

"Yes."

"I really don't mean to pry, children," Eleora Giddings said, and Jasmine cut her off with a bitter laugh.

"Oh, you ain't prying, ma'am. No big deal. Everybody in New Mexico knows about my daddy. Cornwall Dan. That's all I knew him by, all I ever heard him called, but I didn't know him, you see. My mama didn't know him, either. Not really. You see, my mother . . . well, we're not talking about her, are we? Not quite a year ago, vigilantes hanged my father. Hanged him and a cowboy named King. Strung both of them up in the Grant House. But that's all right. I didn't shed any tears over Cornwall Dan's passing. Neither did my mama. Like she won't be shedding any tears over mine."

Curly Bill Brocious's voice rang out: "Hey, Dutch, that girl child, the one you fancy 'cause she don't say nothing, well, she's talking up a storm now. Can't hear what she's saying, but. . . ."

"Shut up, Curly, and watch the walls."

Chuckling, Brocious kicked his feet free of the stirrups to stretch his legs, shifting the Winchester in his arms, enjoying his good humor.

"You're very young to be carrying such bitterness," Miss Giddings said. "All three of you. I don't know you, don't know your father, Ian, or your father, Jack, or your mother, Jasmine, but I bet they love you dearly, and at least you knew all of your parents."

I snorted, the only comment.

Ignoring my sarcasm, Miss Giddings kept on preaching while we walked. "You think of this, children. You were blessed. I never knew my father. Never knew what he looked like, never got the chance for him to rock me to sleep, to tell me stories, never heard his voice, never felt his touch, never felt his love. Think about this."

With another snort, I faced her. "You might want to think about this," I said savagely. "You might want to think about how we're going to get out of Doubtful Cañon alive."

"I think Ringo's right," Ian Spencer Henry said. "I think the Apaches have fled."

My wrath turned to my best friend. "It's not the Apaches I'm talking about, you idiot. Get your mind out of those fool novels you read. It's them!" I hooked my thumb toward Ringo and Brocious.

"Huh? What . . . ?"

"Let's quit that confab!" Brocious ordered. "No more talking up yonder. Just walk."

So . . . we focused on where we were going, twisting and turning into the cañon's depths, past strewn boulders, patches of catclaw and yucca, even a pool of water here and there, through the juniper. Walking . . . following a killer like Whitey Grey, being followed by two more ruthless murderers.

Ahead, the white-skinned man never looked back, making a beeline, plodding on and on.

I noticed it first. Well, maybe not, for Jasmine could have recognized where we were—so could have Miss Giddings—and said nothing. Our location dawned on Ian Spencer Henry, too, and, looking up ahead at the albino, then glancing from side to side, he stopped.

"Hey . . . ," he began.

"Shut up!" I snapped in a frightened voice, fearing my friend would give everything away. I never slowed down. "Keep walking!"

"But. . . ." Ian Spencer Henry obeyed, his face masked with confusion.

"Don't look over there," I whispered when he started to turn his head toward the fort of boulders, behind which lay the graves of Willie Spoon, a Wisconsin gunman called Bruce, and Eleora Giddings's father.

On we walked, away from the buried $30,000, following a half-mad albino, letting him lead us, Curly Bill Brocious, and Dutch Ringo deeper into the cañon.

My eyes locked on the intense figure ahead. I kept going, wondering, praying that Whitey Grey knew what he was doing.

Chapter Sixteen

He vanished.

At the point the cañon twisted around a spot where a chunk of granite the size of Mr. Shankin's mercantile had slid from the northern wall, across what must have been a bone-jarring ride in an old Concord stagecoach, the earth swallowed up Whitey Grey. I stopped, blinking. One moment he had been there. He had turned the corner, and by the time we caught up, nothing stretched before us but the vast emptiness, the solitude.

My gaze shot ahead, then up the cañon's closest side, scanning the rocks for any sign of life. The grade looked too steep, almost sheer cliff, on the opposite side, and, even though the crevassed walls stretched higher in other spots, I just could not fathom how he could have made it even halfway up the rugged walls, couldn't even find a game trail. It would have been hard for a squirrel to scurry up there, forty, maybe fifty feet above, through brush and boulders ready to tumble. He had to be somewhere else, hiding behind a rocky outcrop, a bit of yucca. Somewhere along the trail. Maybe even behind me. But where?

"You kids. . . ."

Dutch Ringo never finished his command. He twisted in the saddle as he rounded the corner, drawing his Remington, looking, and cursing, spurring his mount to the near wall.

"What happened? Where'd that fool man go?" Curly Bill Brocious said, sliding from his saddle to use his horse as a shield.

"Grey!" Ringo screamed.

The echo came back. He whirled, spurred his mount toward a mammoth boulder up the trail, cursed again, loped back, looking one way and the other, keeping his eyes focused on the ground and the low edges of the walls, only daring to look toward the rim when he had ridden back to where we stood. Yet he quickly dismissed that notion, and concentrated on the lower elevations. Who could blame him?

"Grey!" Brocious yelled. "You get back here!"

Ringo urged his horse toward the cañon side, cautious. Sweat dotted his forehead.

"Grey!" Brocious repeated. "I said you get back here . . . now!"

The answer came, haunting.

Grey . . . Grey . . . Grey . . . back here . . . back here . . . back here . . . now . . . now . . . now . . . .

Brocious's sorrel gelding snorted, stamped its forehoofs nervously, and the outlaw spit out a glob of chewing tobacco while Ringo's skittish buckskin danced about. Ian Spencer, Jasmine, and I stood near the fallen slice of granite. A hand pressed on my shoulder, and I let Miss Giddings pull me, and my two friends, close to her.

"Where could he be?" Ian Spencer Henry asked, but no one had an answer.

The report of the Winchester caused me to jump,

and Brocious racked another round into his rifle while trying to calm his jittery horse. He had fired into the far wall, the gunshot reverberating, the bullet whining and whining as it ricocheted off the boulders.

"What are you shooting at?" Ringo yelled. "You see him?" His words bounced down the cañon.

"Trying to flush him out is all." Tugging on the sorrel, fighting the reins, Brocious accidentally pulled the trigger and sent another .44–40 round, this one spanging off a low boulder, clipping another, and burying itself into wet sod underneath the Ringo's horse's hoofs. The buckskin danced in fright, snorting, circling, and Ringo lashed out at Brocious.

"Watch what you're doing, you fool! You almost took my head off!" He jerked the reins savagely, turning the buckskin's head, and, when the mare finally calmed down, or at least quit fighting bit and rein, Ringo looked up, higher this time, searching the shadows and the juniper and, finally, the darkened top.

Nothing. Not even a falcon, just more trees, more rocks, and a cloudy sky.

"You better light down," Brocious said, still hiding behind his horse. "He's got a clear shot at you."

Ringo swore at his partner. "With what? He doesn't even have a gun!"

The boulder, about the size of my chest, crashed inches from Ringo, spooking his horse, which screamed, reared, pawing at the air.

Brocious cursed.

And Ringo fell.

Another boulder. Well, maybe not a boulder, but a good-size rock, heavy enough to have crushed a man's skull.

Like the skies had opened up, raining rocks.

Brocious fired, spooking both horses even more, and the buckskin dragged Ringo, desperately fighting to hold the reins, on his knees, over loose stones, and through a length of mud. "Stop shooting!" he yelled at Brocious, but he needn't have, for Curly Bill had his own problems, now fighting to keep his horse from bolting.

The stone came from the rim. This time I saw it, watched as it arced across the blue sky, then I lost it in the gray and brown of the cañon walls, couldn't find it until after it hit with a sickening *thud*, and the buckskin cried out in terror and pain. It must have hit the horse's croup. She bucked savagely, thrusting her head, and the stone bounced and rolled to the center of the road. Ringo yelled as the leather reins burned his fingers and palms, and slid out of his hands. Kicking, fighting the unseen demon, the buckskin exploded down the cañon, away from us, then shot into a gallop, head down, ears laid back flat on her head, and took off for the San Simon Valley in Arizona.

Releasing a roar of anger and pain, Ringo reached for the Remington he had dropped in the mud, shoved it into a holster, pulled the Thunderer. He winged a shot at the rim, another, and darted to the wall, diving behind a juniper.

"It's your fault, Bill!" Ringo yelled.

Brocious answered him with a curse, tugging his horse up the cañon a few rods, fishing out hobbles from his saddlebag, then cooing at his mount, trying to secure the sorrel's front legs while keeping his Winchester close, trying not to be kicked in the head by his own horse, or crushed to death by Whitey Grey. When he finally had the hobbles on, he wedged himself between an outcrop of rocks and a yucca.

Both men gasped for air, still sweating, nervous, angry, scared.

"You shouldn't have let him get so far ahead, Dutch!" Brocious snapped. "Don't blame it on me."

"I told you we'd gone too far!" Ringo fired back. "I told you that!"

"But you didn't stop that freak, that crazy rapscallion, did you, Dutch? You let him lead us right past that gold, I warrant, let us walk right into an ambush!"

Another rock was launched, and both Ringo and Brocious fired, but we never saw Whitey Grey, no one, just spotted the rocks, the brown against the blue, sailing almost effortlessly, building up speed during the descent, smashing into road or rocks.

"He could be going back!" Brocious said. "Could be going to dig up that gold!"

"Shut up! He won't go anywhere."

"And your horse run off with our whiskey, Dutch!"

"I told you to shut up. Keep your eyes open."

An eerie silence fell upon the bottom of Doubtful Cañon, and a gray cloud hid the sun. How many minutes passed, I'm not sure. Not many, although at the time it seemed like ages. Miss Giddings's hands felt comforting as we watched, waited, wondered.

"He's like those Apaches," Brocious said after a while. "They'd never waste powder and lead on a Mexican. Just stove in their heads by rolling boulders on their heads. By grab, Dutch, we've done that ourselves in this very cañon."

Ringo let out a mirthless chuckle. "Now we know what it feels like."

Another stone tumbled through the air, but this one came maybe twenty yards up the cañon, as if Whitey Grey were running in one direction, then the other, trying to keep the gunmen off balance, which is exactly what he did. The baseball-size brown rock crashed harmlessly against an old cairn, possibly another grave, maybe twenty feet from Ringo's hiding spot.

"You see where that came from?" Ringo asked.

"No! But I think. . . ."

Another rock. Ringo's shot came three seconds after Brocious's. The chunk of yellowish stone smashed ten feet in front of us. We backed up, seeing nothing, not a trace of Whitey Grey.

"How could he get up there?" Brocious yelled. "Must be half mountain goat, that old codger. Or raven."

"Got to be a trail."

"You see it?"

"No. In the shadows maybe, behind one of those trees."

"For a guy as white as he is, that Grey's pretty much Apache, Dutch!"

"Shut up, I say."

Yet Brocious couldn't shut up. I suppose it was nervous chatter. "Maybe he'll run out of rocks," he said. "How many can be up there?"

I felt a tug on my shoulder, craned my neck, saw Miss Giddings, her lips taut, tilt her head to one side. Understanding, I nodded.

A rock sailed. Two bullets fired. And Miss Giddings inched along the face of the fallen section of granite, toward the road. Jasmine, Ian Spencer Henry, and I followed, quietly, slowly, moving around the corner, out of sight of the two frightened gunmen.

I held my breath, but Ringo and Brocious had their minds elsewhere, more concerned with Whitey Grey than their other prisoners.

We kept walking backward a few more rods, three or four steps at a time, then stopping to listen. Gunfire blasted ahead, the echoes booming.

"Now, children!" Miss Giddings spun Jasmine around, pushed her forward, and Jasmine took off as fast as her bum leg would carry her. Ian Spencer Henry and I ran after her, Miss Giddings following us, taking her time, looking back every so often to make sure we were not being pursued.

Curses and gunfire came from around the fallen chunk of cañon wall. Miss Giddings tripped, and I stopped, turned, started back for her, but she had recovered, merely skinning her knees, and told me: "Keep running! I'm all right."

From the other side of the rock, Brocious swore and yelled: "Them kids and that lady! Dutch, they're . . . !"

"Forget them. They can't go far!"

We sprinted down the cañon, away from Ringo and Brocious, away from Whitey Grey, and I felt myself smile as we ran.

Why, that old fool had outsmarted them after all.

Of course, Dutch Johnny Ringo was right. We couldn't go far. We still carried our canteens, but had no food, and only a slingshot and Ian Spencer Henry's antiquated cap-and-ball pistol, which so far had proved ineffective as a weapon. Besides, Jasmine's limp grew more pronounced, and she clutched her left leg as it stiffened.

A shot roared again. Muffled voices. Yet no pursuit.

Not now, at least.

Jasmine slowed, and Miss Giddings said to let her walk, that we all needed to rest.

"Where are we going?" Ian Spencer Henry asked.

Miss Giddings had to catch her breath. "I . . . don't know."

"The ranch house?" Jasmine asked.

"No," I said. "They'd look there. We can keep on walking, out of this place, back to Stein's Peak station. Those velocipede cars are there . . . maybe. . . ." Doubts again. What if Southern Pacific officials had discovered our plunder and confiscated the stolen handcars? There was no water at Stein's Peak, and we didn't have enough in our canteens to make it back to the *Playas*. Besides, for all I knew, the water in *Valle de Las Playas* had dried up by now anyway.

"We'd be out in the open," Ian Spencer Henry said, and I knew he was right. "And Jasmine can't walk that far. Look at her now."

Resting on a rock, she bit her lip, gently massaging her ankle, saying nothing.

"The house." Miss Giddings's head bobbed.

"But," I argued, "that's the first place they'd look."

"I know, Jack," she said. "But remember . . . they threw my rifle, the one Mister Spoon gave me, out the front door. It still shoots, the stock's just busted. And they threw the other rifle out there, too."

"Mister Grey's Colt, too." Ian Spencer Henry liked her idea, whatever it was. "I don't think they picked up any of those guns. Might have, but I'm certain sure they didn't get those rifles."

"We couldn't fight those men," I complained. "That's Johnny Ringo and Curly Bill. They're killers. They'll gun down every last one of us."

Eyes flaming, Miss Giddings raised her voice, and

almost waved a finger in my face, stopping herself at the last moment. "We don't have any choice, Jack! We have to go to the house, get those guns."

Jasmine let out a little sob. Her head shook, and she dropped her head. "I don't think I can make it to the house. That's at least two miles from here." She brushed away a tear. "Y'all leave me here."

"We're not leaving you!" I said angrily. "If I have to carry you. . . ."

"You're not going," Miss Giddings said. "None of you shall go to the house. Like Jack said, that's where they'll look."

I felt confused. "But you just said. . . ." I started, only to be interrupted one more time by my best friend.

"We can't stay here!" Ian Spencer Henry looked at the sky. "It'll be dark soon. Well, not soon, but . . . well, soon."

Miss Giddings glanced up the cañon, then down, wet her lips, and offered a faint smile. "You can stay here. All of you. I'll go to the house, get the guns, hurry back." Another smile, even weaker than her first effort. "With luck, maybe Ringo and that other man, maybe they've given up. Rode off up the cañon, trying to find Ringo's horse. I don't think either is so hungry for gold. I think they're both scared."

"Not Curly Bill Brocious," Ian Spencer Henry said. "And sure not Ringo."

"Ringo the most," she said. "He's scared of dying. Petrified. Scared of his own mortality. I've never met a man as scared as he is. You saw it, Jack." Her eyes held mine, but I didn't know what she meant. "When you told him he'd be dead in two or three years. He went straight to the bot-. . . ."

Both of our eyes fell as we thought about my father.

"You were very brave, Jack." Miss Giddings tried again. "Very brave."

"Then I should go for those guns," I said.

"No." Her head shook.

"Maybe we don't have to," Ian Spencer Henry said. "Like you said, ma'am, maybe Ringo and Brocious turned yeller and ran. Rode double. Got out of the cañon, went on to Arizona." His head nodded as the idea grew on him. "Yeah, that's what I think. So we're safe."

"No, Ian." Miss Giddings was the only person I ever knew who called him only by his first name. "We have another person to consider, and I don't think he's about to give up his search for that money."

I mouthed his name. *Whitey Grey.* Then I said: "I'll go. You three hide. I'll come back for you. I promise."

Yet Miss Giddings would not relent. A Shakespeare mule could not match that lady's stubborn streak. "No, Jack," she said. "Again, no. But thank you. I'll go. You children hide."

"But where?" Jasmine asked.

She grinned again. "I know just the spot."

Chapter Seventeen

With Jasmine leaning on my shoulder, we slowly covered another three or four hundred yards, then dipped through the maze of fallen boulders and squeezed through the little opening. Ian Spencer Henry had called our natural redoubt a fort, and it probably had saved our lives when the Apaches had attacked a day earlier.

Limping only slightly now, Jasmine reassured me: "I feel fine, Jack."

So did I . . . until I saw the graveyard.

"Wow," Ian Spencer Henry said tightly, "would you look at that. . . ." His voice trailed off.

You couldn't help but look, because even though I wanted to turn away, I couldn't. Open-mouthed, horrified, I just stared, blaming myself. We hadn't given Willie Spoon much of a burial, hadn't had time, once the Apaches hit us, to cover his grave with stones the way the freight men had done over the two other graves twenty years earlier.

After muttering a prayer—or starting one, at least—Miss Giddings shielded Jasmine's eyes, but that maternal act didn't last long either, for she realized the hopelessness of it. Instead, her long arms dropped to her sides, and she caught her breath, tried to fight back the choking sobs.

"Poor. . . ." she said. "Poor, poor Mister Spoon."

His rib cage and skull lay close to the dug-up hole, the rest of his bones scattered across the area. No blood, no flesh, just bones, stark and empty, not quite bleaching but haunting nonetheless.

"They picked him clean," Ian Spencer Henry said to no one in particular, sounding a lot like Whitey Grey, and turned to me. "You reckon Apaches done it, Jack?"

My head shook. Like many other men I had known, Whitey Grey called the Apaches practically fearless, except when it came to darkness and death. They didn't even like to speak of the dead, and to touch them . . . well, I had seen the look on the Chiricahua boy's face when he had leaped on me. It had been a face of strength and brutality, even after I had shattered his nose, until he rolled into the grave and had seen death so close. He had cried out in fear, and only then did he turn and run. We hadn't whipped that Indian, not by any stretch of the imagination. Willie Spoon had won that battle for us, won it in death.

And this is his reward?

The thought shuddered me, but I managed to answer Ian Spencer Henry. "Wolves, I guess. Ravens." I looked skyward. "Maybe buzzards. Ants."

"That's gross," he said.

"Yeah. It is."

"Come on, children." Her courage returning, Miss Giddings led us through the feasting ground, careful not to touch any of the strewn bones.

"Shouldn't we . . . ?" Jasmine swallowed. "Shouldn't we bury . . . what's left?"

"No time," Miss Giddings said. "Later maybe. Later, certainly. But first I want y'all to hide. And stay put." She turned the corner around a clump of catclaw, her eyes searching the cañon walls.

"You looking for the cave?" Ian Spencer Henry said. "The gold?" No doubt about it, the buried fortune occupied his thoughts. My friend couldn't keep from studying the cañon, tripping over rocks, and almost walking into a yucca plant, wetting his dry lips, scouting for that tree that marked the location of the treasure.

Not that he was alone in that pursuit. Honestly I felt my own eyes trying to find that sliver in the ground near the alligator juniper—at least for a while—with about as much success as I would have had looking for a sober man at Falstaff's Tavern. The thought, the imagery shattered me. I pictured my own father, in his cups, in front of that bucket of blood back in Shakespeare. I saw him begging Dutch Ringo and Curly Bill for a coin, anything to slake his thirst.

"Watch where you're going, Ian!" Miss Giddings called out, but she didn't heed her own advice. She stopped, leaned against a chalky boulder, squinting her eyes, shaking her head after a couple of minutes before moving on, slowly, deliberately.

The wind blew in a sudden gust, bringing the chill in the air. Since the rainstorm, the air had turned cooler, reminding the desert that autumn had arrived.

"There!"

Miss Giddings pointed, but it took a moment for the slit to register. "That's it," she said, scrambling up the rocks, kicking loose a river of dust, pebbles, and cactus spines. "This is where I hid from the

Apaches. At first, I mean, after. . . ." Stopping, she knelt and held out her hand. Jasmine took it, and Miss Giddings pulled her up. Ian Spencer Henry and I climbed up ourselves, without help, and eased our way into the opening.

"Mister Grey might have hid here, too," Ian Spencer Henry said, then frowned. "I hope there ain't no tarantulas in that hole."

"I'm not sure a spider could fit in there," I said, but the crevasse was misleading. With Miss Giddings's help, Jasmine slipped into the small cave, and Ian Spencer Henry and I followed, but not before she pressed a canteen in my hand.

"Take care of them, Jack," she said. "Stay alert." She pointed. "You've got a good view of the cañon from here. Don't make a sound. Don't answer to anyone till I come back. Just be still and quiet. You can see out, but it's hard for anyone to see inside, so you'll be safe. I'll be back as soon as I can." She hesitated, found the sun, bit her lower lip. "It might be morning." She listened, but we hadn't heard any noise in the longest time. No gunfire. No horses. No Apaches or Curly Bill Brocious or Dutch Johnny Ringo.

"I've got Pa's Colt, ma'am," Ian Spencer Henry said. "I'll take care of my friends."

She smiled, sad but sweet, and her nod lacked confidence. "I know you will, Ian. Jasmine, will you be all right? How's your leg?"

"Better," she answered. "I'll be good as new with a little more rest. Just walked too much today."

The rock walls felt cold, and I tried not to shiver. Whether or not Miss Giddings returned, we would have a long walk. Two miles or so out of Doubtful Cañon, another six or eight to the Southern Pacific tracks . . . in hard country, with Apaches and outlaws on the loose. I shook the canteen, testing the water. Miss Giddings carried the other canteens.

"I'll fill these at the spring," she said. "Get the weapons, come back. But like I said, it might be morning. I couldn't find this place in the dark."

Then she did what struck me as odd. She slipped into the opening and hugged us, I mean a bear hug, almost forcing the air out of my lungs, kissed Jasmine's forehead, and climbed out. I watched her until she disappeared, then leaned back into the creeping darkness.

"Jack?" Ian Spencer Henry asked.

"Yeah?"

"You don't reckon she's going to leave us here? Do you?"

After the sun sank, I thought about Ian Spencer Henry's question. Earlier I had scoffed at my friend's suggestion—so had Jasmine—but with the cold and dark blanketing us, listening to the wolves and coyotes, reservations about Eleora Giddings entered my mind.

Would she return? I mean, why? She'd have enough water to get to Stein's Peak, could handle one of those George S. Sheffield & Company velocipede cars as well as we had. We'd just slow her down. She'd have weapons, and, most importantly, she'd be out of Doubtful Cañon. Why would anyone return? Walk two miles into one of Southwest's most treacherous cañons, then another two miles to get out. She'd witnessed all this country had to offer, had seen how it had killed her father. Come back? To save three children she didn't even know?

Once more, a wolf sang out, and a dark cloud swallowed the moon.

I woke stiffly after a fitful night of bad dreams, none of which I could remember clearly as dawn broke with drab gray skies and a bitter, persistent wind. After craning my neck to stretch the aching, tight muscles, I stepped out of the entrance and looked.

Nothing. No sound but the wind. Nothing to see but the confines of the cañon, the bleakness of desert. I sank back into the shadows, trembling.

"People disappear all the time," I remembered my father telling me when we had first settled in Shakespeare, on Halloween if I recalled correctly. "Out there." Smiling at me, winking at my mother, he had pointed westward. "One moment they are living, breathing individuals, full of hope and foibles, and then they are like the dust, maybe they are dust, their memories, their lives, just blown away and forgotten." He had tousled my hair. "Apaches claim some, *banditti* many others, but I suppose most are just driven away by the land itself, killed from exposure, Nature, thirst, sickness, even madness." He'd snapped his fingers. "Like that." Another smile and another wink. "So be careful, my boy. Don't let New Mexico swallow you up."

Ian Spencer Henry blew on the cylinder of his Colt, and looked up at me. "You reckon Injuns waylaid Miss Giddings?" he asked.

"I don't know."

"I heard a lot of commotion over yonder way." He gestured toward the burial ground.

"Wolves," I said, and shuddered at the thought of Willie Spoon's bones. "Or coyotes."

"I thought I heard horses, too." He shoved the pistol in his waistband.

The sound of hoofs came back to me, and, recalling the noises of the night, I looked up and down the cañon again. Had that been a dream? I wasn't sure.

"I'm hungry, Jack," my friend said.

Jasmine echoed his statement. "Me, too."

"How's your leg?" I asked her.

"Better."

"Can you walk?"

"Sure."

Ian Spencer Henry rose, his right hand gripping the revolver's butt. "Then let's go."

I shook my head. "We wait," I said, "for Miss Giddings. Just like she told us to do."

So, we waited, our stomachs growling, the wind rustling through the rocks and juniper, whipping the remaining moisture from the cañon.

And waited. . . .

"She ain't coming, Jack," Ian Spencer Henry said. "She run off." His head shook. "No, no, I don't think she'd do that. She took a shine to Jasmine. She wouldn't leave her." He frowned. "But maybe the Cherry Cows got her."

Waiting . . . even when I knew Eleora Giddings would not return. We waited and watched until the walls of the little slice in the rock closed in on me, and I darted out of the confines, into the noon light, and hollered at my comrades: "Come on, let's get out of here!" The echoes of my voice startled me, but I refused to retreat.

What was I supposed to do? Stay in that hole until

we all died, died of starvation, linger until we turned to dust to be blown away and forgotten?

"What are we going to do?" Jasmine asked after I helped her down off the rocks.

"The same thing Miss Giddings planned," I said. "Go get those guns, fill this canteen at the spring, backtrack our way to Stein's Peak, and wait on the next Southern Pacific train. Westbound or eastbound, I don't care."

Just get out of this country.

I started walking, not even slowing down when Ian Spencer Henry called out in a hushed but urgent whisper: "But, Jack, you're going the wrong way."

"First," I said, "we rebury Mister Spoon's bones."

Strange, my preoccupation with giving Willie Spoon a decent burial. My friends sure found it odd, that obsession. Not that I could explain my reasoning, if indeed it was reasoning to them. Not that I even understood my actions myself. My father's words kept dancing in my head: *One moment they are living, breathing individuals, full of hope and foibles, and then they are like the dust, maybe they are dust, their memories, their lives, just blown away and forgotten.* I pictured Willie Spoon in that shallow grave, watching his face turn into my own.

Something else my father had once said also came to me, more words that I could not clear from my troubled, tired mind.

"In the end, Jack, the only thing a man has is his conscience. Forget about money, home, fame, any of that stuff. Nothing matters," he had told me.

"What about his word?" I had asked him.

He had shook his head. "A man's word doesn't mean anything without his conscience. That's a man's being. That's a man's worth. That's why some men do the right thing, and why too many others don't. Some men will do the wrong thing, but, in the end, they'll make it all right . . . if they have conscience."

I kicked a stone savagely, rocketed it twenty feet into the cañon wall. *What happened to your conscience, Pa?*

"What's that, Jack?"

I blinked away my tears. I didn't realize I had said that aloud. "Nothing," I told Jasmine. "We're almost. . . ."

We were there, and I stopped, gasping.

Willie Spoon's bones were gone. The grave remained uncovered, bits of cloth that I hadn't noticed the previous day here and there, but I found no bones, nothing left of Willie Spoon except dust. My heart sank.

"It must have been the wolves," Ian Spencer Henry said.

The wind kicked up even harder, kicking up dust, and Jasmine's voice quaked when she asked: "Can we get out of here now?"

I didn't answer, just looked. *We should have buried those bones yesterday. No, no, Miss Giddings was right. We didn't have time, couldn't chance it.* I stopped debating myself, tried to tuck away those doubts always plaguing me. Sighing, I looked at the yucca near the graves. I caught my breath again.

"What is it?" Ian Spencer Henry said.

"The spade." A shaking finger pointed at the desert cactus. "The pickaxe," I said. "They're gone."

We had left them behind, after the Apache ambush. Closing my eyes, I tried to remember, picture the details. Evening. The albino had crawled to us.

Leave the pickaxe and that spade here, by ol' Willie Spoon's grave. Whitey Grey's wild drawl sounded clear in my mind.

"Apaches must have took them," Ian Spencer Henry said.

"Maybe," I said, but again I heard Whitey Grey. *Don't reckon 'em Cherry Cows'll touch it. . . .*

I looked up, catty-corner from the graves, and the mirage came to me, as clear as the white-skinned man's words.

A deathly pale figure came sliding down the cañon, flowing along the loose gravel and dirt as if canoeing through the rapids toward a waterfall. Tan-colored duck trousers were stuck inside battered boots of different sizes, different colors, though it was hard to tell from all the dust on the leather, and he wore grimy braces over a plaid bib-front shirt missing several buttons, not to mention the green and white bib. An ancient calico bandanna kept his hat, the ugliest, dirtiest thing I'd ever seen, from blowing off, the kerchief wrapped around the crown, pulling the brim over his ears, knotted underneath his chin. He carried no gun that I could see, balancing himself on his descent with a pickaxe in his right hand and a broken spade in his left.

He landed in a cloud of dust, fell sideways, and jumped up, his joints *creaking*, tossing the tools into the dirt and running for us, those wild eyes beaming, thick white mustache dancing like a snake on his upper lip.

"By jingo, it's you!" the mirage said with a snort as he slid to a stop near the empty grave. "My chil'ren! My ol' pards! Y'all's come back to help Whitey Grey find his gold!"

Only . . . he was no mirage.

Chapter Eighteen

First, he jerked the canteen from my hands, pulled out the stopper, and drank greedily, allowing precious water to stream down his whiskers, dribble off his chin. Smacking his lips, Whitey Grey shook the canteen around, belched, and handed the empty container back to me.

"That's good. Good," he said, while I gaped, imagining the wind sucking the canteen's lip dry. "I sure needed that. Don't worry, young 'uns, we can gets more water at the spring. It's just two miles yonder, maybe a li'l' more. Water's good, though my druthers would be for somethin' with more bite. Had some yesterday. Water. Not whiskey. We'll gets more. But first. . . ." He gestured toward the cañon wall.

I didn't follow his arm. I stared straight ahead at him.

"What happened?" I said. "Back up the cañon? When you were throwing rocks down on Ringo and Curly Bill?"

His arm fell to his side, and those hollow eyes blinked rapidly several times. After wiping the water off the ends of his flowing mustache, he asked: "What you talkin' 'bout, boy?"

"You were throwing rocks down from the rim," I said, and Ian Spencer Henry added with an exclamation: "You sure scared the living daylights out of Dutch Ringo and Curly Bill! Scared them good! Us, too."

The albino's head shook. "No. Wasn't me. Was 'em Cherry Cows that done it."

"What?" my friend and I blurted out together. "I thought. . . ."

The albino's massive head rocked from side to side. "Nope." At last his lips turned upward in a crazy grin, and he chuckled. "You thunk I climbed the wall up that cañon?" Slapping his thighs, scattering dust, he laughed even harder. Dutch Ringo said Whitey Grey was insane, and I agreed. The man belonged in the Tucson asylum. "Nope," he said. "Can't be done. Climbin' 'em rocks. Not there nohow. Not by me. 'Specially iffen Apaches is up there. You gots to go around, come up from the other side of the cañon, gets to the rim that way, lessen you's part mountain goat, which I ain't."

"But . . . ," Ian Spencer Henry began. He stopped, trying to remember the events of the previous day, finally turning to me for help.

Yesterday I had been certain Whitey Grey had been on the rim, hurling rocks from the heights like some human catapult, scoring hits, running off Ringo's horse. I wasn't alone. Brocious and Ringo had been certain those rocks had been launched by Whitey Grey. Everyone had. Who else could it have been?

I hadn't even considered Apaches.

The white-skinned man grunted. "Tol' you 'bout 'em Apaches, how they likes to throw rocks down on folks comin' through this here cañon. Save 'em some powder and lead. Guns ain't cheap. Bullets neither. And 'em rocks hurt, boys. Quiet, too."

Ian Spencer Henry's head bobbed slightly. "Yeah, Dutch Ringo and Curly Bill said they've done it, too. On Mexicans."

"Sure, sure." The albino tousled Jasmine's hair, smiled, smacked his lips some more. " 'Em Cherry Cows ain't gots no patent on rock tossin'. Would've done it myself, 'ceptin' a body's gots to be more limber and younger than this ol' hoss's. No." He bellowed again. "You ain't joshin' ol' Whitey Grey, is you? Really? Ringy and Curly, that trash, they really thunk it was me poundin' 'em with rocks?" Another thigh slap, another cloud of dust. "By my boots and socks, that's bully. Just bully."

"We all did," I told him.

He patted my head, almost knocking off my stolen cap. "No," he said. "It happened this way, chil'ren. You see, I rounded that bend in the cañon, where that hunk of cañon fell off years, years ago. And here comes a rock. Plunk! Barely misses my head. Well, I knowed it was Cherry Cows, knowed what 'em red devils was up to. So I hurried back to that slice of cañon, the one that was partly blockin' the road, been blockin' it as long as I can recollect. And I found me a place to hide in the corner. Make it harder for some rock to bash in my thick head.

"That's where I was. And then, here come you chil'ren, so I snakes back in that little slit, and up rides 'em two lyin', cheatin', thievin', slanderin' murderers and rakes, Ringy and Curly Bill. That's when 'em Cherry Cows let's 'em have it. Good fight. Liked to have stayed, yes, sir, I surely would, stayed and watched it, but it strikes me that, by grab, I can slip right through that rock. There was this openin', you see, betwixt that chunk and the rest of the cañon wall. Hard to gets through, but 'tweren't no impossibility. So I done it. And then I taken the ankle express and run all the way back to that ranch house." He nodded, stopped, frowned. "Well, I didn't run all the way. Run till I got tuckered out. Then I walked. Figgered to gets me a good drink at the spring, pick up my repeatin' rifle and six-shooter. Anyhow, I come back here to spend the night."

"The guns!" I cried out.

Jasmine followed my thought, asking: "Did you see Miss Giddings?"

It took Jasmine three more tries before the name finally registered.

"That petticoat?" the white-skinned man asked dumbly. "You mean to tell me 'em Apaches didn't stove in her head?"

"No," Ian Spencer Henry replied. "She led us away. Curly Bill and Ringo were too occupied with the stones coming down on them. She took us here. Then over yonder that way. Told us to wait, that she'd come back for us probably this morning, only she didn't."

"She went for the guns," Jasmine added. "Took our canteens to fill, too. You sure you didn't see her?"

"She. . . ." The albino blinked with wonder. "She went for 'em guns?"

"Yes!" we cried out.

"Well, I'll be. . . ." His head bobbed in approval. "Lady's gots sand, gots more gumption than her ol' man, and Mister Giddings had a belly full of it. Might've mentioned that afore. I respected her pa."

I bit my lip to keep from saying something I would regret. *Respected her father? You killed him!*

"But you had to have seen her?" Jasmine said, her

voice fraught. "You would have passed each other . . . right?"

"No. Not so that you'd knowed it," the albino explained. "Likely she crept along this side of the cañon. Me? I snaked along the other side, like we done the first time we come into Doubtful." He snorted, and wiped his nose with his hand. "If we heard one another, I warrant she thought I was some Apache buck and I kept quiet, figgerin' she was the same. Like ships passin' in the night. Ain't that how the sayin' goes? 'Course, it wasn't night, not then, not when I come back anyhows. And we ain't ships . . . not in this terrible ol' desert. Speakin' of ships and desert, though, I could use some more water. I'm a mite thirsty."

"You drank the last of it," I bitterly informed him.

"Well," he said, "we gots more pressin' matters. We can gets water later."

"She wouldn't have left us," said Jasmine, her face masked with concern over the fate of Eleora Giddings. "I know she wouldn't have left us."

"No. Likely not." The albino scratched dust-caked beard stubble on his chin. "Ringy might have grabbed her, though. Wouldn't put it past him. Wouldn't put nothin' past that scalawag. Or his pard."

That led to another question. What had happened to Ringo and Brocious?

"I'd hoped 'em bucks would've stoved in their heads," Whitey Grey told us. "Didn't work out, though. Some time past midnight, I reckon. Maybe afore. Dark anyway. Dark and cold." He pointed to the rock fortress. "I was gettin' a li'l' shut-eye over yonder, and hear this hoss a-lopin'. One hoss. Two men on its back. Couldn't make 'em out, not as dark

as it was with 'em clouds and all, but I taken it to be
Curly and Ringy."

My heart sank. I pictured Miss Giddings, bravely
walking back for us in the darkness, being surprised
by those two outlaws. Then I pictured something
else.

"What about the Apaches?" I asked urgently.

He shrugged. "They's gone. Now I been hopin'
that for a spell. 'Tain't worked out that way, yet. But
I can't imagine 'em stayin' put here for this long.
Apaches likes to keep movin'. I'm bettin' they played
their last hand again' Ringy and Curly. They's
young, green when it comes to fightin'. Like up yonder yesterday. They got anxious. Tossed that rock at
me. A full-growed Apache, he would have waited
till we'd all rounded that bend, then launched the
ambush."

Changing the subject, I pointed at the open grave.
"What happened to Mister Spoon's bones?"

"Wolves and coyot's gots 'em," he answered matter-
of-factly. "I seen that last night, even as poor as my
eyes can be. Reckon they dug him up. You chil'ren
should've put stones on that grave!"

I ignored the admonishment. What had he done?
And we were a trifle busy.

"No matter," he continued. "They had a regular
feast, come back last night for 'em bones to gnaw on.
Which reminds me. I'm hungry. You chil'ren gots
any grub?"

"We're hungry, too," Ian Spencer Henry said.

Jasmine stomped her foot, ignoring any pain in
her legs, and shook her head angrily. I'd never seen
her so furious. "Why are we standing around here
talking about food and water, none of which we

have on us." She pointed down the cañon. "We need to go after Miss Giddings. Something must have happened to her!"

The white-skinned man ignored her. "Gettin' chilly," he said. "Maybe I'll head down to Yuma when I gets my gold. It's warmer there. Hot, actually. They don't know the meanin' of the word cold." He frowned, shaking his head. "No, no, not Yuma. I gots my belly full of Yuma." He looked at Ian Spencer Henry. "You ever been in the prison there?" Not waiting for a reply, he went on. "Well, don't go, iffen you can helps it. Got a big prison in town now, too." He lifted his head, pondering other options. "Maybe the Sandwich Islands. Or Mexico. Don't speak much Mexican, but I do like tequila."

My head shook as I stared into the lunatic's eyes. I'd never met anyone as crazy as Whitey Grey.

"What about Miss Giddings!" Jasmine screamed into the wind.

Whitey Grey stared at her as if she were an ant. "Don't worry 'bout that petticoat," he said, and tugged on his mustache. "Woman with that much gumption, she'll be fine . . . iffen she ain't already dead." He straightened to his full height, nodding as if answering some question he had asked of himself. "The point is, she ain't here. Not now. Ringy and Curly Bill ain't here. Not now. I ain't seen no sign of Apaches, so maybe they's gone, too. We's here. And so is my gold!"

Gold! I'd almost forgotten about that $30,000.

"Did you find it?" Ian Spencer Henry asked.

Jasmine just stood there, her face red with anger, her body shaking.

Ever the peacekeeper, I interrupted the albino and

Ian Spencer Henry, suggesting that perhaps we should return to the house, refill our canteen—the one canteen we had left—and check on Miss Giddings. We couldn't abandon her. But Whitey Grey would hear nothing of the kind.

"I done tol' you. We be here. My gold's here. I ain't traipsin' up and down Doubtful Cañon no more."

This time I didn't hold back. I caught another glimpse of Jasmine, saw her about to lash out at our leader, but I stepped out first, telling him firmly: "No, sir. Miss Giddings comes first. We have to save her. Find her!"

His backhand took me by surprise, and the next thing I knew I was on my backside, my lip bleeding, Jasmine kneeling beside me, both of us staring into those haunting eyes of a soulless man.

"My gold," he said. "One day, chil'ren, you's gonna learn that I'm ramrod of this here outfit. We's gettin' my gold."

"Did you find it?" Ian Spencer Henry repeated, his voice soft, his body trembling, eyes moving from the white-skinned man to me.

With a sigh, the white-skinned man sank, melting into the ground, knee joints popping again. "Well, chil'ren, there's one problem I've learnt." He pointed up the cañon side. "The tree's gone."

This time I followed his outstretched arm, looked at the incline where Whitey Grey had slid down back into our lives. Unlike most of Doubtful Cañon, here stood loose rock, packed on a little hill before flattening into the hard granite that lifted skyward, bleak and dark. From the albino's story, I recalled, Mr. Giddings had dropped the saddlebags of gold into a narrow opening, marked by an alligator juniper, but up on that ridge, the land was as barren as much of the desert. Some cactus, and even those looked half dead, but no juniper.

"Been gone for years, I reckon," Whitey Grey said sadly. He offered a hand, and pulled me to my feet, forgetting, it seemed, that he had knocked me to the ground. Jasmine and I kept a respectful distance.

Mad. Crazy. Insane. Unpredictable. A monster.

"You sure this is the right spot?" Ian Spencer Henry asked, his voice still timid.

Only Jasmine kept her strength, her determination. Stepping away from me, to protect me, I guess, she roared again: "What about Miss Giddings?"

"Yonder's the grave," the albino said, scratching his chin. I don't think he even heard Jasmine's shout. A gust of wind blasted us again, grew stronger, more persistent, and Whitey Grey had to shout to be heard. "Right there's where we buried Mister Giddings, and we planted him pret' much where he fell! And I could see that ol' tree when we was havin' his funeral, so it was there. Up yonder! But it ain't there no more! Looked all mornin', I done, and looked a lot yesterday, too. No sign of it. Not even no roots. No trunk. Nothin'. See how that side's. . . ."

"MISS GIDDINGS!" Jasmine's shout seemed to stop the wind if only briefly, and her echo boomed off the cañon wall. "We can't abandon her."

"Quiet, li'l' girlie," Whitey Grey said. "I'm talkin' here. You see how that side's caved in some? Slid down. Rock slide. Avalanche. Flash flood. Who can tell, but when that chunk of ground give way, it must've taken my tree with it. Then probably some greenhorn come by and chopped it up for firewood. By grab, it's been twenty years."

"You mean . . . ?" Seeing his dreams of a fortune

in half-dime novels vanish, Ian Spencer Henry gulped. "You mean the gold's lost?"

"No. No. No." The albino's voice rose with confidence, or reassurance, with every syllable. "No, it's there, by grab. It's gots to be there. Just the openin' is buried 'neath that dirt." He started walking toward the side, and obediently we followed him, even Jasmine, though, from the shade of her ears, her temper had not lessened. "No," Whitey Grey said, stopping at the edge. "No, my gold's still there."

The wind started again, moaning, and I had to hold the stolen cap on my head. I looked at the sky, searching for signs of a storm, but found nothing but gray clouds.

"What do we do?" Ian Spencer Henry asked.

"First," Jasmine demanded, "we go find Miss Giddings."

Shaking his head, the albino picked up the shovel and pickaxe. "No. First . . . you dig."

The pick was shoved into my hand, the spade into Ian Spencer Henry's. Whitey Grey grinned. "Up yonder."

Jasmine muttered something, whirled, and started for the rock fortification. "You do what you want," she said, "but I'm going to find Miss Giddings."

She didn't stop until the Apache leaped over one of the rocks and blocked her way. Then, she screamed.

Chapter Nineteen

You'll probably think I'm lying, but it really happened this way. Staggering back from the approaching Apache brave, Jasmine fell on her backside, no longer screaming, but crabbing her way on hands and feet from the menacing figure. Whitey Grey blurted out: "Confound it, they's back! 'Em Cherry Cows is back!" And he bolted for the rocky redoubt, leaving Ian Spencer Henry and I standing there, twenty yards from Jasmine and the young Chiricahua.

Me? Well, I think I shouted something heroic—like "Watch out, Jasmine!"—and couldn't move. Brandishing a war axe, the Apache boy made a bee-line for Jasmine, lifting the club over his head. The wind moaned, and the next noise deafened me. Standing like one of the stalwart subjects of his beloved half-dime novels, Ian Spencer Henry pulled that relic of a Colt from his britches, thumbed back the hammer as he aimed, and squeezed the trigger. This time, the .44 didn't misfire, but detonated the percussion cap that ignited the black-powder cartridge and sent a piece of lead into the Chiricahua's left thigh.

"Hey!" shouted Ian Spencer Henry, shocked as any of us, with the exception of the Apache. "I hit him!"

Yelping in pain, the Indian dropped the axe over his shoulder and fell backward. Only the boulder kept him from tumbling to the ground, and, as the pungent scent of gunsmoke brought me back to motion, sending me charging to rescue Jasmine, and Ian Spencer Henry thumbed back the hammer to chance another shot, the young brave—not the same one who had attacked me earlier, for this one's nose wasn't flattened—turned and limped through the opening, disappearing moments before the Colt's hammer struck with a metallic click.

"Confound it!" Ian Spencer Henry lamented.

"RUN!" I yelled over my shoulder.

Jasmine recovered, rolling over and leaping to her feet before I reached her, and she took off for our rock fort, diving in beside the albino. I followed her, and moments later Ian Spencer Henry stumbled in, landing on his back, raising the old pistol, looking for another target.

The wind died down, and we heard the guttural chants of the Apaches. Cautiously I looked over the top of the natural redoubt, but couldn't see the Indians, couldn't fathom a guess as to how many there were, five or fifty.

"Why don't they charge?" I asked.

"Surprised 'em," the albino said. "Figgered we didn't have no guns, but they'll come directly and finish us off. Hear 'em. They's workin' up their courage, singin' their death songs. Don't know we only gots one gun."

"One?" I shouted. When the white-skinned man ran here, I had assumed he was heading for his cache of guns. "You said you got your Colt and Winchester when you went back to the rock house!"

Blinking rapidly, he studied me a moment before

shaking his head. "You wasn't listenin'," he said. "I said that was my intention. Wanted my Colt and repeater and some water. The water I drunk. Only the guns wasn't there. None of 'em." He hooked a thumb toward the Apaches. "They got 'em first."

He didn't explain further, but I sorted out a theory. The Apaches had watched us from the hills. Preferring to strike from ambush, they knew better than to charge the rock house, where we'd have plenty of cover. When we had left, prisoners of Brocious and Ringo, the Indians had picked up the two abandoned rifles and pistol. Most of them backtracked their way out of the cañon and worked their way up to the rim, dashed ahead to surprise us around the bend in Doubtful Cañon. They wouldn't have used their newfound weapons, not at first, because, as Whitey Grey kept saying, Apaches cherished powder and lead, and boulders and stones often worked just as well. Maybe a few stayed behind, anticipating, if any of us survived the catapult ambuscade, that we'd retreat back to the rock house by the spring.

My heart sank.

That, I thought, had been Eleora Gidding's fate. Maybe Brocious's and Ringo's, as well.

"Tarnation," Whitey Grey said. "This close to my gold, only to be kilt by 'em Cherry Cows."

Ian Spencer Henry, buoyed by his marksmanship, said: "We ain't dead yet."

"Yeah," the albino said. "We are. Lessen you think you can hold 'em all off with that thing." He pointed at my friend's old revolver. "Criminy, boy, it only works one time in ten. Nope, chil'ren, we's kilt . . . certain sure."

Dead, I thought, *and all my fault*. I would be responsible for the deaths of my two closest friends. I'd pay the price, too. I looked out to the makeshift grave-yard several yards away. If we were lucky, I thought, we'd wind up like Mr. Giddings and the gunman named Bruce. If not . . . we'd be like poor Willie Spoon, our bones winding up in some coyote's den.

Hopeless. Still fixed on the graves, I reached out and took Jasmine's hand, squeezing it.

"Let's run then!" Ian Spencer Henry said.

The albino's head shook. "Make a run for it, and they'll cut us down. That's what's keepin' 'em at bay, right now. Only way they knows to gets in here is through that li'l' hole, but they gots to finish the fight now. So they'll come."

"But we can run. . . ."

"No, no. Just get cut down, I done tol' you," the old man repeated. "And I figger if I gots to die, might as well die here, close to my gold."

"We can hold out till dark." Ian Spencer Henry refused to give up. "Like we did before."

"Sundown's a long time comin'," Whitey Grey said. "They won't wait that long. Ain't got much experi-ence, 'em young bucks, but they's eager to prove 'em-selves. And we's been lucky. Had 'em boys knowed better, they'd have waited till we all rounded that bend, then ambushed us yesterday. Gots lucky is all. That first rock could've crushed my head. Lucky then. Lucky when 'em bucks hit us here, too, that first time. Onliest reason we didn't get kilt then was 'cause that boy attackin' Jack fell on that dead man."

Dead man. I focused on the open grave. Willie Spoon, I remembered thinking earlier, had saved us in death.

"Spooked 'em, it did. Apaches be scared of the dead," I heard the albino say, "but they ain't afeared of dyin'." He sighed, resolved to his fate. "Nope. This time, it's all over but the dyin', screamin', and buryin'."

I released Jasmine's hand, jumped up, and grabbed the albino's strong arms, pulling him, saying something insensible, telling him we had to get to that grave. My friends stared at me, thinking I had lost all reason, but I shot out: "It's our only chance!"

"What you talkin' 'bout boy?" Whitey Grey refused to stand.

"The grave!" I said. "You get in the grave. When the Apaches come. . . ." I couldn't think. "Like Lazarus."

"Who?"

"Lazarus?" Jasmine said, not repeating my statement, for she sounded just as confused as the white-skinned man.

"There's no time to explain," I said. "We've got to hurry."

Apache voices had grown louder. They'd be coming soon. To kill us. Yet maybe we could save ourselves, with luck, counting on that Apache dread, their superstition.

At last, Ian Spencer Henry understood, and he shoved the Colt into his waistband, and joined my assault on Whitey Grey, trying to make him stand, force him into the opening, to the hole in the earth where we had tried to bury Willie Spoon. "Rising from the grave," my friend said. "It could work."

No, it couldn't, I thought, *but what other chance do we have?*

Jasmine helped, and finally the albino rose, but stopped before we left the rock fortress.

"You ain't buryin' me in no grave!" he said. "Not yet." His words fell to a whisper. "It's bad luck."

"Bad luck?" I snapped. "You're crazy. This is our only chance! We're about to be killed, you fool! Scalped!"

His head shook. "Cherry Cows don't scalp, Jack. You knows that."

Jasmine kicked him in the butt, and he relented and headed for the grave. We ran, and he ran with us, suddenly changing his mind, mumbling that yeah, that my plan had possibilities. "And iffen it don't work," he said, "at least I'll be in a grave when I'm kilt."

He slid into the grave, and frantically we kicked and covered him with a loose mound of dirt, keeping his face clear, hoping the Apaches wouldn't notice it. "When I give the signal," I told him, "you stand up. Like Lazarus."

"Never met the fella," he said.

I swore, heard a falcon cry, dashed to the edge of the cañon, hiding behind a yucca near the sandy hill, near Whitey Grey's gold. I saw a flash of red headband, knew the Apaches were coming, and my doubts returned. That entrance wasn't the only way here. Easily the Chiricahua could creep along the cañon's edge, as we had done. They could make their way to the top of the rim on this side of Doubtful, crush us by rolling boulders over the precipice. They could stand behind the strewn boulders forming the maze and shoot us from there.

My idea . . . it was horrible.

The first Apache boy came through the opening, the same one whose nose I had broken with the blunt shovel, followed by two more, one holding a bow, an arrow already notched, another with the late Willie Spoon's Henry rifle. The first brave held the stolen Colt. We were dead.

Jasmine knew it, and she screamed.

Yet that shriek prompted Whitey Grey to climb out of the grave, the howling wind scattering the dust and dirt. The sight even unnerved me, for here rose this ghost, a white-skinned abomination, with stark white hair, coughing out the sand he swallowed, snorting, dancing, yipping like a banshee.

The Apache with the Colt yelled, turned, and retreated, stumbling over the other two, forcing his way through, running, leaving the others staring in horror at the ghost climbing out of the grave. One of those began his own death song, dropped the Henry, turned, fled. The last Chiricahua wasn't far behind.

They vanished. Whitey Grey kept pounding the dirt off his body, brushing away the touch of the dead. Jasmine, Ian Spencer Henry, and I stood watching, struck dumb by the sight and the sound of thundering hoofs as the Apaches fled Doubtful Cañon.

"It worked," Jasmine said incredulously.

That's when I heard scattered shots, and more hoofs.

"Or did it?" Ian Spencer Henry said.

The next sound was the blaring of a trumpet.

"The Army!" Jasmine yelled, and she took off running. Screaming, shouting with joy, Ian Spencer Henry and I ran after her, leaving the crazy old albino doing his dance, purging himself of sand from his ears.

Short-lived was our relief.

Oh, we stood there for a while, cheering as dust-coated black men galloped past on their horses, although I admit a strange feeling that I hoped the Apache boys would escape. I mean, my father had once told me that the Indians were fighting for their land, and these weren't horrible killers, not to me at least. Well, they hadn't killed me. Besides, they were just boys. Like me.

One of the black soldiers tipped his slouch hat toward us as he rode by, a Springfield carbine in his hand, and we cheered harder. Even Whitey Grey, who had joined us, muttered some respect. "Never thought I'd be so happy to see a bunch of blue-bellies," he said. He raised his voice to a shout. "Go get 'em, you Yanks!" Then, squinting and stepping back, he told me in a whisper: "Jack, 'em's colored fellas."

"Ninth Cavalry," said a white officer as he trotted to us on a blue roan gelding. "From Fort Bayard. I am Lieutenant Skylar Gaugy."

His horse pranced about as more soldiers thundered past, and the young man—with his pale face and mustache of peach fuzz, he didn't look much older than me—had trouble controlling his mount, which wanted to take off after the others, yet he managed to grin at us. "Your mother and father are alive, children," he said. "They'll be relieved to see that you and your grandfather are likewise."

My mouth dropped. *What on earth . . . ?*

Said Whitey Grey: "Huh?"

"Both of your sons are alive, sir." The officer addressed the albino, and he turned back to the column as a covered wagon driven by one black soldier veered off toward us, followed by another soldier on a high-stepping gray horse.

"What's he talking about, Jack?" Ian Spencer Henry said.

By then I knew. At least I felt it in my churning gut before the soldier driving the wagon set the brake, before the corporal on the gray horse held back the canvas at the rear of the wagon, and a woman jumped down.

Eleora Giddings started for us, but a voice stopped her. Two more men climbed out of the wagon, and I knew who they were before one grabbed Miss Giddings's arm and led her toward us, smiling.

"We pulled your daughter-in-law and your sons from the house at the entrance of this cañon," Lieutenant Gaugy said. "Three Apaches had pinned them there, but we ran those Indians off. It gladdens my heart everyone's alive. We've seen too much death already. I'm sure your hearts are joyous, too."

Beside me, as the blue roan snorted and almost unseated the lieutenant, Whitey Grey snorted and mumbled something about *sons*.

Chapter Twenty

For a moment, I contemplated warning Lieutenant Gaugy and the two troopers, but Miss Giddings's pleading face told me to stay quiet. She was right, I guess. Pretending to be my father, Curly Bill Brocious put his right hand on the butt of his revolver while his left pinched Miss Giddings's arm like a vise. Beside them walked Dutch Johnny Ringo, his thumbs hooked in his shell belt, cold eyes blazing with arrogance, daring us to try anything.

Two other wagons lumbered by, followed by a half dozen more cavalrymen, all disappearing up Doubtful Cañon.

"Mister Witsenhauser," Lieutenant Gaugy addressed Brocious, leaving me wondering how the man-killer had come upon that alias, "we have these renegades on the run. I must join my troops."

"Understood, Capt'n." Brocious and Ringo stopped just in front of us, never looking back at the lieutenant.

"I'll leave Corporal Merchant and Trooper Muller with you."

Ringo suddenly frowned. "There's no need for that. . . ."

"There most certainly is," the officer said. "I not

only have a duty to my command, sir, but to a higher
duty, a moral one. The Apaches ran off your horse,
and this country is no place to be afoot . . . not with
three young children and a young woman. Or. . . ."
He wet his lips, trying to think of a polite term for
Whitey Grey. I prayed the officer would realize the
brigand's deceit, but to no avail. "Your father," Lieutenant Gaugy said at last. Tugging the reins, he
turned the horse around and barked orders to the
two black soldiers, issuing orders to escort us as far
as Lordsburg, then return with haste to Fort Bayard.

The soldiers saluted, and the corporal stepped
down from his mount, wrapping the reins around
the wagon wheel.

"Ma'am," Lieutenant Gaugy said, tipping his hat
and bowing slightly, "keep your homecoming short.
Gentlemen, children. Good luck!"

He spurred his horse and galloped after his command, leaving us with two grinning gunmen and a
couple of soldiers who didn't know their com-
mander had likely just ordered them, plus the rest
of us, to death.

"Luck," Whitey Grey said with contempt, and spit
in the dirt.

Brocious shoved Eleora Giddings forward, urging
her to—"Go see our young 'uns, Mama."—and with
a dry laugh he turned back for the wagon, offering
to help Trooper Muller down. An old man, his hair
and beard as white as the albino's, the black soldier
protested, but Brocious insisted. Meanwhile, Ringo
had walked over to the corporal, a younger man,
heavy-set for a horse soldier, hooking his thumbs in

his belt, striking up a conversation about chasing Apaches.

"Thanks," Trooper Muller said, breaking away from Brocious's grip. The old man started to tip his battered slouch hat in an amicable greeting, but never finished. Curly Bill Brocious clubbed the kind cavalryman with the barrel of his Russian, and the soldier cried out and toppled forward, his head barely missing a jagged rock.

"What's this . . . ?" Corporal Merchant started, but Ringo silenced him with a sickening *thud*, using the barrel of his Thunderer, and the big man dropped without a sound.

"Should I kill 'em now, Dutch?" Curly Bill stood over the unconscious Muller, pointing the cocked .44 at the man's bloody head.

"No," said Ringo, stepping over the fallen corporal and walking back to us. "I don't want those soldier boys to hear any shooting."

"I could slit their throats."

Ringo shook his head, smiling at us. "Just tie them up, Curly."

He didn't fool me. He was trying to lull us into some security. By sparing their lives, he figured we might think we had a chance to get out of this mess alive. I knew better. Once they had that fortune, they'd kill us all.

"You get your gold, old man?" Ringo asked, though he never took his eyes off Miss Giddings and me.

"It's gone," the white-skinned man answered. "You was right, Ringy. Waited twenty years for nothin'. Somebody else must've found it."

Ringo's face remained unreadable. I understood card players considered him a tough opponent at a poker table. He started to speak, still staring at us, but stopped when Curly Bill Brocious cried out that he needed a hand. Swearing, Ringo pivoted, warning us to stay put, and helped his partner hog-tie and gag Corporal Merchant and Trooper Muller, then drag, drop, and shove both men, still knocked cold, into the back of the covered wagon. After dusting themselves off and sharing a drink of water from a canteen, the two gunmen came back to us.

Ringo never hesitated, never lost that smile that had returned. He drew the long-barrel Remington, thumbed back the hammer, and placed the barrel against Jasmine's temple. Miss Giddings whirled, calling him a miserable coward, reaching for his gun hand, but Curly Bill Brocious grabbed her around her slim waist, pulled her back, and threw her onto the ground, then aimed his own revolver at her head. Ian Spencer Henry and I just stared, uncertain. Whitey Grey tugged on the ends of his mustache. Jasmine bit her lip, but stood bravely, unflinching.

"I'm out of patience, Grey," Ringo said. "Where's that gold? Or I'll blow this child's brains all the way to Mexico."

"It's . . . ," I started, but Whitey Grey's heavy sigh silenced me, and I watched him step back and hook a thumb.

"C'mon," he said, and led us through the rocky maze into the opening, past the graves. Stopping at the cañon wall, he pointed up the hill.

"I don't see no hole," Brocious said.

"Something happened." The albino explained how some force of Nature had removed all sign of the cave, including the juniper. The wind picked up again, cold and stark, kicking up dust devils that quickly died. I shivered, and Miss Giddings snapped at the killers that we needed water and food. Absentmindedly Brocious tossed her the canteen before fingering a bit of peppermint candy from his pocket and throwing that in the sand, too.

"You sure this is the right spot?" Ringo asked.

"Yeah." Whitey Grey thumbed at the graves. "That's where we planted this lady's pappy." His jaw jutted up the hill. "It's thereabouts. Somewheres."

"Let's get out of here, Dutch!" Brocious shouted over the wind. "It ain't worth it. That hole could be filled in with dirt, and we could spend a week digging without ever finding a thing. And this crazy old guide we have ain't exactly reliable. Besides, more soldiers might be coming. Or 'Paches."

Ringo studied the hill, unblinking.

"Come on, Dutch! It ain't worth it, I say!"

"Not yet," Ringo said calmly. His smile returned, as did the life in his eyes, and he kicked the broken shovel with the toe of his new boot. When he faced us again, he dug a thumb-size bit of jerky from his own pocket and placed it in Ian Spencer Henry's hand.

"Eat up," he said cheerily. "You'll need your strength. All of you." He pointed his revolver at the tools. "Eat up. Then start digging."

We dug, Ian Spencer Henry swinging the pickaxe, Whitey Grey clawing with his fingers, me using the broken spade, Eleora Giddings and Jasmine pushing rocks down the hill or carrying them to the edge. The wind didn't help things, and soon my mouth felt dry, but I knew better than ask for a drink or stop toiling.

Below, squatted Curly Bill Brocious and Dutch Johnny Ringo, both of whom had pulled their bandannas over their mouth and nose to keep out the blowing dust.

We dug, until our hands were blistered, until I thought everything futile. The sun had almost dipped behind the rim, and the wind turned even colder. I wondered if Ringo would realize the hopelessness of our venture, and worried what he would do when he called it quits. Ian Spencer Henry had grown weary of the pick, handing it to Whitey Grey while he pushed away stones with his hands, and, when that grew tiresome and painful, he began kicking them with his heels.

We dug.

And then Ian Spencer Henry scrambled to his feet, staring at sand spilling into the earth, and shouted: "Hey!"

That brought the two killers out of their slumbers, and they dashed up the hillside, while the rest of us gathered around my friend's discovery. "I just kicked that rock out of the way, it was real heavy, and the sand started falling away," he explained.

"G-g-g-give me that pickaxe!" Ringo managed after jerking off the bandanna from his face. He ripped the tool from the albino's hands, then began pounding the ground, cursing, breathing heavily, finally stepping aside as Curly Bill Brocious and Whitey Grey fell to their knees to dig with their hands, breathlessly, excitedly.

After a few moments, they stopped. Ringo pitched aside the pick, and Curly Bill Brocious pulled himself up, removing the bandanna from his face. Whitey Grey remained on his hands and knees, peering into the emptiness of a tiny hole.

"Is . . . is that it?" Brocious asked.

Silently the albino reached into the hole, his white hand disappearing, and began tugging at something. A *snap* followed, and he brought out a piece of dead wood.

"Juniper root," Ringo said softly.

"This is it!" Whitey Grey said excitedly. "My gold. This is where Mister Giddings dumped his saddlebags." He looked up, his eyes pleading at Miss Eleora. "It gots to be!"

Ringo struggled for composure, tried to think, kept pointing away from the hill. "The wagon," he said at last, and pushed Brocious. "Go back to that Army wagon. Get a rope." He wiped his mouth with his sleeve. "Fetch that rope. There's a lantern, too. Remember? In the wagon. Hurry!" He whipped off his hat and dropped to the ground beside the white-skinned man. "Hurry. Get moving, Curly!"

For the next few minutes, no sound came except the heavy panting of the men and the wailing wind. The light had begun to fade into the gray of approaching dusk, and suddenly Ringo laughed and slapped Whitey Grey's back. "You were right, old man," he said. "Only a kid could get through that hole."

Brocious came running back, the lantern swinging in his left hand, a coiled rope over his right shoulder. He climbed up the hill, cursed as he slipped and slid down, then regained his footing and made it to the small cave.

"Might be snakes," Ringo said.

"Uhn-huh," Brocious answered. "How deep you think it is?"

Ringo's head shook. He looked around, grabbed a stone, and dropped it in the hole. The *thunk* came a few seconds later. "Not that bad," he said. "I don't know. Fifteen feet? Twenty? Fire up that lantern." He pulled himself up, took the rope, stared at me.

"Pay day, gents," he said. "Which one of you children want to fetch our gold?"

"I will."

Ringo blinked, staring at Jasmine Allison, who stepped forward. "I'm the smallest," she said.

"Ringo," Miss Giddings said, "you can't. You can't send a child in there. It could be a rattlesnake den. You can't. . . ."

"She volunteered, ma'am," the gunman said smugly. "And we can't get through that hole. You neither, even as skinny as you are."

"But. . . ."

"Can't blast the hole any bigger," he went on. "Nearest dynamite's in Shakespeare, and an explosion could bury everything. I fancy getting out of this cañon before dark, ma'am."

She stammered, but before she could argue further, Dutch Johnny Ringo smiled. "Ma'am," he said gently, "your pa died for what's in that hole. Don't you want to see it?"

He slipped the rope under Jasmine's shoulders, secured it, tousled her hair, and handed her the lantern Brocious had lit.

"I'll see that you get an extra dollar, kid," Ringo told her, "if you find the gold."

"What's it look like?" she asked.

"In saddlebags," Whitey Grey replied. "Brown. Had Mister Giddings's initials burned in the leather on both sides." The albino frowned. "Lessen Mister Giddings dumped it all out."

"It's gold," Curly Bill said dreamily. "Heavy, beautiful gold coin." He took the end of the rope, locked his feet in the sand, bracing the rope around his back. "Watch for snakes," he said, and Dutch Ringo helped lower Jasmine Allison into the pit.

Miss Giddings caught her breath. I wrung my hands. And Jasmine Allison disappeared out of sight.

Brocious grunted as he lowered the rope, with Ringo at the entrance, helping feed the line.

"Can you see anything?" Ringo called out.

"No!" came Jasmine's muffled voice.

"How 'bout you, Dutch?" Brocious said through clenched teeth. "Can you see . . . ?"

"Nothing."

We waited, holding our breath, nervous. Brocious stopped lowering the rope, loosened his grip, and stepped forward. "I think. . . ."

"I'm at the bottom!" Jasmine called up.

Ringo cupped his hands over his mouth, spacing his words deliberately. "Can you see anything?"

"It's all dusty and dirty down here," she said. "And tiny."

"Tell her to turn up the lantern," Brocious whispered to his partner.

Ringo ignored his advice. "Those bags," he yelled down, "they are probably covered with dirt! Rocks! Back when the ridge washed out. You might have to dig it out!" He turned rapidly, pointed at me. "Grab that shovel, boy. Hand it to me." I obeyed and he dropped it into the pit. He was too excited, too impatient, too thoughtless to tell her his intentions.

"Hey!" she snapped. "You almost hit my head!"

"Sorry," Ringo said. He wet his lips. The wind died down, as if waiting, also, for the $30,000.

We listened to the far-off sound of Jasmine working in the pit. Ringo rose, turned, sank to his knees, stared into the blackness of the hole, stood again, sighed.

"Let's send in another kid," he told Brocious. "Help her dig."

Nodding, Brocious grabbed my arm and shoved me at Ringo.

"I need the rope," Ringo told Jasmine. "We're bringing it up." He thought a moment and added: "Honey."

"Wait!" Jasmine screamed.

"It's all right!" Brocious yelled. And to Ringo he said: "Tell her we're sending her some help."

Ringo's head bobbed again, but Jasmine cried out: "I think I've found it!"

Brocious shot out a Rebel yell, and Ringo smiled triumphantly. He dropped back to his knees, looking inside the opening, and spoke clearly: "Tie your end of the rope to the saddlebags! Are . . . did you . . . is it in the saddlebags?"

"Yes. It's heavy."

Another war cry. Brocious fell beside Ringo, then both men rose. "Let us know when you've got the rope on those saddlebags!" Ringo hollered. "Tie a good knot!"

"It's ready!" Jasmine yelled. "But don't you forget to send that rope back down for me."

Brocious's laugh came up short when he gave the rope a tug. Grunting, grimacing, he strained as he and Ringo pulled, tugged, then shouted: "Help us!" Whitey Grey dashed forward, and Ian Spencer Henry and I started, but Miss Giddings grabbed our shoulders, keeping us near her.

They pulled. Pulled. Ringo let go, fell back on his knees and reached inside with both hands. "Just a few . . . more . . . got it!" He fell on his stomach. "Keep pulling, you fools! Don't drop it! Pull!"

Dust-coated, worn leather came through, the bags bulging, buckles broken. Miss Giddings relaxed her grip, and we all gathered around the saddlebags, watching Whitey Grey brush dirt off the dried leather until the faint tracing of a brand burned into the hide became legible: J J G.

Softly Miss Giddings repeated her father's name.

"Hey!" Jasmine called out. "Get me out of here!"

Brocious started to gather the rope, but Ringo stopped him.

"Don't bother," he said in a wild whisper, and, straining, pulled open one of the bags and dumped out its contents.

Chapter Twenty-one

A deafening, savage curse exploded from Dutch Johnny Ringo's mouth, and he jerked the Thunderer from its holster, slamming the barrel against the back of the white-skinned man's head. Whitey Grey, who had crawled forward to stare at his treasure, pitched forward, planting his face in the pile of rocks.

"You idiot!" Ringo roared, kicking at the old man, aiming the revolver at the albino's back, thumbing the hammer, shaking his head, cursing again. "Twenty years!" he yelled. "For this?" The pistol boomed, its report echoing in the approaching darkness, spitting sand into Whitey Grey's open mouth. The albino sat up, clutching a chunk of granite in each hand, staring blindly, blinking, mouth open, blood running down the back of his head, sticking to that flowing mane of white hair. "Fool!" Ringo said, and started to pull the trigger again. "Rocks! Rocks! Nothing but rocks. You idiot!"

Curly Bill Brocious just stared, bewildered, and finally let out a little groan.

"What's going on?" Jasmine's voice called from inside the pit. "Don't you leave me here. I want to get out! Throw me the rope! What's going on up there?"

Ringo laughed coarsely, kicked the pile of rocks, shoved the revolver into its holster. "Twenty years, you've waited, Grey. Twenty years . . . for dirt. Which is what you are, old man. Dirt. You're as worthless as these rocks." He spit, pushed back his hat, and swore again. "And I'm just as worthless for hitching my team to your wagon. Idiots!"

The granite slipped from the albino's hands. Pale eyes fluttering, he just sat there as the blood flowed.

"Maybe. . . ." Curly Bill ripped open the other bag. "Maybe. . . ." He reached in, pulled out. . . .

"Yeah, Curly." Ringo turned away, shaking his head, his lips tight, knowing what his partner would find in the other pouch.

Brocious picked up the saddlebags, dumped out more dust, rocks, and filth, then, swearing, he flung the ancient leather at Miss Giddings's feet. "I told you, Dutch . . . ," he began.

"Shut up, Curly. Shut up, or I'll fill your gut with lead." Ringo laughed again, his voice hoarse.

Silence returned for a minute, broken by Whitey Grey's snickers. "Mister Giddings," he said, nodding with respect. "Man had a belly full of gumption. Come all this way with bags full of rocks. Rocks. By jingo, I must've had rocks in my head."

"That gold could be anywhere," Brocious said numbly.

"Don't think it ever left Texas," the white-skinned man said. "Not with Mister Giddings nohow. Reckon we was a decoy. Mister Butterfield and 'em Overland boys probably had other arrangements. But . . ."—he grinned at Miss Giddings—"your pappy had sand, lady. He wouldn't turn back, wouldn't shirk no duty. He died for the Overland. Sure played me for a fool. He. . . ." He turned toward the noise.

Ringo heard it, too, filling both of his hands with revolvers.

"Horses," Brocious whispered urgently. "Might be the Army. If they find them colored boys in that wagon. . . ." He started down the hill, calling over his shoulder: "The game's up, Dutch! Come on!" Muttering an oath when Ringo refused to budge, Brocious stopped at the bottom of the hill. "We got one horse, that Army horse, Dutch! Unless you want to take that wagon through Doubtful! Come on, will you! The pickings have got to be easier in Tombstone!"

Whitey Grey kept laughing, and Ringo began making his way down the hill, but on a whim he stopped, whirled, and aimed the Remington at my chest.

"They ain't worth it, Dutch!" Brocious gave up, running for the maze.

The wind had started again, not as violent as before, as I looked down the barrel of that heavy .44.

"Ringo!" Miss Giddings gasped.

His face looked dead, and he cocked the hammer. I closed my eyes. A body stepped in front of me, and, when I pried my eyelids open, I stared at the bloody back of Whitey Grey's head. "Ain't you a big man, Ringy," I heard the white-skinned man say. "Killin' a kid. Ain't I more your size?"

Metal *clicked*, leather *creaked*, and Ringo's voice called out with a dry laugh and low whisper: "Curly's right! You ain't worth it."

With that, he was gone, racing down the hill, across the opening, and through the rocks.

Whitey Grey loosened his bandanna and placed the sour-smelling rag against the gash in his head, sat down, and sighed. Hoofs thundered, followed by a scattering of shots, more hoof beats, shouts. Miss Giddings took off toward the old Overland road, lifting her voice, yelling for help. My knees buckled, and I sank onto the earth, Ian Spencer Henry dropping beside me, his hand steadying my shoulder.

"You all right, Jack?" he asked. "I thought you was dead, for sure."

From the pit beneath us, Jasmine cried: "If you don't get me out of this hole, you're gonna be real sorry!"

I made myself move, needed to work, to get the image of Ringo's pistol out of my head, so Ian Spencer Henry and I grabbed the rope and dropped one end into the black hole while Whitey Grey started singing some old song, stanching the flow of blood with that rag, rocking, laughing, talking to himself. We pulled, Jasmine shouting her instructions, and finally her right hand shot out of the hole. I knelt forward, grabbed it, and we lifted her back into the dusk, hugging her.

"What happened?" she asked.

I started to answer, but a woman's high-pitched voice stopped me.

"Jasmine!" We spun around, watched in stunned silence as Berit Ann Allison charged forward, lifting the hems of her calico dress, tears of joy flowing down her face. "Jasmine! My love!"

Jasmine blinked, dropped the rope in the dust, and took a tentative step forward. "Mom?" she said.

More faces and figures appeared in the maze, led by Miss Giddings, who pointed up the hillside toward us. Mr. Shankin came through, and many others. One man in a tan, sack coat stumbled, tossed aside a Sharps rifle, and pulled himself up. "Ian!" he hollered. "Boy?"

"Pa!" Ian Spencer Henry showed no hesitation. He raced down the hill, slid to a stop, charged back up, and grabbed the canvas war bag that carried the old Army Colt. Then he hurried back down the hill, and sprinted for his father. Jasmine got her legs to work, and, tears welling in her eyes, she ran into her mother's waiting embrace. I stared at the opening, searching the faces, and staggered beside Whitey Grey, squatting beside him.

I didn't see my father.

Well . . . I hadn't expected to. Not really. I mean. . . . What did I mean? A tear broke free, rolled down my cheek. Then another. And another. Until I made them stop.

Whitey Grey's callused hand patted my knee. He had stopped singing. "You're a good boy, Jack Dunivan," he said. "A mighty fine pard!"

Sniffing, I wiped my eyes, took a deep breath, and watched Mr. Shankin climb up the hill, out of breath, followed by several other men from Shakespeare, miners and merchants, some that I knew, many more that I didn't.

"You gave us all quite a start . . . ," Mr. Shankin began. He knelt beside me. "You all right? You look as if. . . ."

"I'm fine," I lied.

Rough hands jerked Whitey Grey to his feet, started shoving him down the hill. "This is the one we want," a voice said. And another: "The fiend!" Still another: "Fetch that rope!"

I wiped my eyes again, oblivious to the tumult around me. "How'd you find us?" I asked.

"Those two men from Lordsburg," he said. "And we found those railroad cars at Stein's Peak. It wasn't. . . ."

"Hang him!" another voice cried out. "Child stealer. Thief! String him up the way we did Cornwall Dan . . . !"

The shout died, and I looked in time to see the man's head drop. Others stared uncomfortably at Berit Ann Allison and her daughter, but they didn't seem to hear or notice, just wrapped themselves together, sobbing in joy.

"Come on, Jack." Mr. Shankin held out his hand, and I took it, letting him pull me up. For some reason, I grabbed the old saddlebags, lighter now, but still spilling dust, and followed the mercantile owner down the hill. Two more figures emerged from the maze, Trooper Muller and Corporal Merchant, the former holding a wet cloth on the back of his head, the corporal rubbing his wrists where the bindings had chaffed the skin.

"Curly Bill and Ringo?" I asked.

"Who?" Mr. Shankin said. "You mean the two . . . ?" His head shook. "Got away. Didn't know who they were. We would have gone after them, but they were riding deeper into the cañon, and then this woman said . . . well . . . we wanted you, to find you."

"Where's a tree!" someone yelled.

"Let's just shoot him. Here's a half-dug grave we can use."

"He don't need to get buried, not the likes of him!"

Another voice came, this one softer, and I looked, my knees buckling, the tears coming again. This time I made no effort to stop crying.

"Pa!" I yelled, dropping the empty saddlebags.

And ran for my father.

He had stayed behind to help the soldiers in the wagon, maybe dreading what he would find, fearing me dead. I buried my face in his chest, felt his strong arms squeeze me, heard him crying as well. I didn't smell liquor, only dust and sweat. I didn't feel chagrined, only love.

He sobbed. "I . . . promised . . . made a vow . . . I said if you weren't killed . . . I'd never . . . never . . . I'd never touch whiskey again." He hugged me tighter. "I'm sorry, Son. I . . . I'm. . . ."

"I'm sorry, Pa," I said.

Other voices grew louder, and I pulled myself away from my father's embrace, fisted the tears from my eyes, sniffing, making myself stand and face these men bent on lynch law.

"Leave him be!" I yelled, surprised to hear Ian Spencer Henry echo my own orders. He joined me as we marched toward Whitey Grey, his hands now bound behind his back, a rope around his neck.

"He saved us!" Ian Spencer Henry said. "He stood in front of Jack, wouldn't let Ringo kill him. Stopped Ringo from killing Jasmine, too. He saved us all!"

It was a stretch, perhaps. Or maybe not.

"Let him go!" This time my father barked the order. "You hang this man, you harm him, I will print every last one of your names in my newspaper. In every paper in the territory. You'll be branded as murderers, just as you should have been branded when you took the law in your hands before, when you hanged Cornwall Dan and Harley King. There will be no lynching here. Let him be!"

With muffled voices, they stared.

"Let him go," Berit Ann Allison said.

Even Miss Giddings stepped forward, demanding the release of the white-skinned man.

"Here." Mr. Shankin pulled a handful of crumpled bills from his vest pocket. "Here's fifty dollars, mister. Take it and be gone. Get out of our sight, out of New Mexico Territory. Turn him loose, boys."

The rope came off, as did the bonds around his wrists, and Whitey Grey dusted himself off, pulled on his hat, and grabbed the money before Mr. Shankin or anyone could change his mind. He shoved the greenbacks into his pocket, came to Ian Spencer Henry and me, and patted our heads. "You's good pards," he said.

"Start walking!" one of the miners thundered.

The albino winked, and told us in a whisper, "Don't y'all fret none. I knows where 'em centipede cars be. I'll be fine, pards. Look me up sometime." His eyes found the saddlebags and he picked them up, started to toss them over his shoulder. "Reckon I spent twenty years huntin' this. So I deserve it." He looked inside one of the pouches, squinting, pursing his lips, and reached inside. He pulled out something small, dusty—I couldn't make it out—studying it, and then, throwing the saddlebags over his shoulder, walked to Miss Giddings and handed the battered daguerreotype to her.

"Warrant your pappy didn't want this to fall in no Cherry Cow hands, neither," he said. "Can't blame 'im none. She be a right handsome woman. Takes after you."

Tears formed in Eleora Giddings's eyes as she stared at the faded picture.

"Mama," she whispered as Whitey Grey, whistling some bawdy tune, walked into the desert.

We camped that night in Doubtful Cañon. Well, the bulk of the posse headed out, some opting for a grog shop over in the San Simon, most riding back to Lordsburg or Shakespeare. The two soldiers, Mr. Shankin, and our parents stayed in the rocky fort, figuring it was just as safe as the rock house, and the soldiers, their heads throbbing, were in no particular hurry to go anywhere. Well, that's the reasons everyone gave anyway. Mostly I think they wanted to give Miss Eleora Giddings time at her father's grave.

She stayed with us, too.

We told our story. Our parents explained how they had found us. The men Whitey Grey had way-laid along the Southern Pacific tracks had tipped them off. No one had ever found the note I had planted. They hadn't even thought about looking in the Lady Macbeth Mine—so much for my genius, I figured. Instead of thinking we were running away for El Paso, they had believed that this crazed albino seen in the town's saloons had kidnapped us, and the posse had left Shakespeare, vowing vengeance.

I felt weak. Our foolishness had almost gotten several people killed—including us. Even Whitey Grey had almost been lynched, which, many people in Shakespeare would later say, he should have been.

"Well," Mrs. Allison remarked over the campfire. "No harm done."

"Yeah," my father agreed. So did Ian Spencer Henry's.

Lucky we were. Under other circumstances, all of our hides would have been tanned for such transgressions.

We supped on hardtack, biscuits, beans, bacon, and salt pork, slept well, and rose early. Mr. Shankin started frying bacon and boiling coffee, while Ian Spencer Henry's dad recounted the story we had told him, shaking his head, scoffing at our youthful stupidity for chasing gold.

"Buried treasure," he said with a snort. "I hope you have learned your lesson."

"Pack of lies," Mr. Shankin agreed. "I told you as much back in my store, Jack."

"Yes, sir," I agreed.

"Well. . . ." Jasmine pressed her lips together, and began nervously playing with her fingers. She kept glancing back to the pit, then at her feet. Finally with a heavy sigh, she unlaced her left shoe, pulled it off, and reached inside. What she removed sparkled in the morning sun.

Mr. Henry let out an oath, and, embarrassed, quickly apologized.

"I wasn't going to tell anyone." Jasmine looked at Ian Spencer Henry and me. "Except you. Later. Thought we might come back. . . ."

"There's more?" I blurted out, my eyes locked on the gold coin.

"All of it," she said, and let out a giggle. "I reckon. I mean those saddlebags were full of sacks. One broke open."

Miss Giddings scratched her head. "But. . . ."

"I didn't want those men to have it," Jasmine said. "I mean, I found the bags as soon as I got down there, but Curly Bill and Ringo would have murdered us if they got their hands on that money. Maybe they would have killed us even if they didn't. I. . . ." Like a little girl, she shrugged.

"Down . . . ?" Mr. Henry gulped. "Down there?"

The soldiers came over, staring at the glittering coin. Corporal Merchant whistled. My father remained silent, close to me, smiling.

"How . . . how much?" Mr. Shankin asked.

"Thirty thousand," Miss Giddings replied.

Looking up, Ian Spencer Henry did a quick head count. "Ten of us. That's three thousand dollars each. Easy to do in my head."

"Oh. . . ." Mr. Henry coughed. "No . . . I mean . . . that . . . well, the Overland Mail . . . that money would belong to. . . ."

"John Butterfield's dead," Mrs. Allison said.

"And Wells, Fargo and Company isn't missing that money," her daughter added.

"More money than we'll ever make soldierin'," Trooper Muller said.

"But how do we get it?" asked Corporal Merchant.

"You got to go down in that hole," Ian Spencer Henry said. "But it's only big enough for one of us kids. That's why Jasmine went down yesterday." He grinned. "Can I go this time? I want to go. Please." He paused as we gathered around the little hole, ignoring the burning bacon and the coffee boiling over. "There wasn't no snakes down there, was there, Jasmine?"

Smiling, she shook her head. "No spiders, either."

Mr. Shankin wet his lips. "Then let's get it out. In a hurry. Get it out and get out of Doubtful Cañon!"

"Amen," murmured Trooper Muller.

Mr. Shankin and Mr. Henry gathered the rope, and Ian Spencer Henry, beaming, bravely stepped forward. They slipped the rope over him, secured it beneath his armpits. "Be careful, Son," Mr. Henry said.

"Hey!" My best friend suddenly found me. "You don't mind if I go, do you, Jack? I mean . . . well. . . ." His voice lowered. "Do you want to go?"

"You go," I said.

"You sure it's all right?" he asked, eyes excited once more.

I felt my father's hand on my shoulder. "It's fine," I said, smiling. "Everything is just fine."

Author's Note

Buried treasure stories are plentiful throughout the Southwest, and the legend of John James Giddings hiding the Overland Mail Company's $30,000 before being overrun and killed by Apaches in Doubtful Cañon is one of them.

This much of my novel is based on fact. According to New Mexico historian Marc Simmons, Giddings and four men—three guards and the driver—came across the ruins of Stein's Peak station and were later attacked by Apaches almost the moment they entered Doubtful Cañon. The driver and one of the guards were shot off the top, and the runaway team took off, overturning the stagecoach two miles into the cañon. What happened afterward is open to speculation.

Teamsters discovered the scene a few days later, the stagecoach riddled with bullet holes and arrows, and the remains of two men nearby. Wolves and vultures had reduced the bodies to nothing more than skeletons, one of which was believed to be that of John James Giddings. Both were buried in the cañon. The third man was never found, and thus he became my fictitious Whitey Grey, named by my then-four-year-old son.

In 1917—not in the 1880s as in this novel—
Giddings's daughter sought out the grave of her father. Two Texas ranchers helped her find the site,
and eventually she put a stone marker over Giddings's grave. Folks say it's still there today.

John James Giddings, Born June 30, 1821. Killed
by Indians April 28, 1861.

Shakespeare remains standing as a ghost town
today—although a 1997 fire destroyed part of it—
open to tourists on select days. Stein's Ghost Town,
right off the Southern Pacific rails, is also around
for visitors along the Arizona-New Mexico border.
Interstate 10 bypassed Doubtful Cañon, even more
remote these days than it was in the 19th Century.

Johnny Ringo and Curly Bill Brocious did roam
Shakespeare and the Doubtful Cañon area in the
1880s, so I thought they would serve well as my vil-
lains, although I don't really think either went out
looking for buried treasure in October of 1881. Their
legend and infamy, of course, grew in Tombstone
shortly after my story ends. The fates of both men
are still debated by historians.

In addition to Simmons, I also should thank the
Bureau of Land Management's Las Cruces and Pe-
cos districts, which oversee the Doubtful Cañon
area; writers Fred Grove and Melody Groves, for
sharing information about Doubtful and Stein's
Peak station; Emily Drabanski and Terry Tiedeman
of *New Mexico Magazine*, for tracking down an old
article about Doubtful; and the following books:
Ghost Towns and Mining Camps of New Mexico by
James E. and Barbara H. Sherman (University of
Oklahoma Press, 1975); *The Civil War in Apacheland:*

Sergeant George Hand's Diary edited by Neil B. Carmony (High-Lonesome Books, 1996); and *The Butterfield Trail in New Mexico* by George Hackler (Yucca Enterprises, 2005).

The $30,000 (or $28,000, according to some sources) Giddings allegedly buried has never been found. Maybe it's still there in Doubtful Cañon.

Or maybe . . . just maybe. . . .

Johnny D. Boggs
Santa Fé, New Mexico

About the Author

Johnny D. Boggs has worked cattle, shot rapids in a canoe, hiked across mountains and deserts, traipsed around ghost towns, and spent hours poring over microfilm in library archives—all in the name of finding a good story. He's also one of the few Western writers to have won two Spur Awards from Western Writers of America (for his novel, *Camp Ford*, in 2006, and his short story, "A Piano at Dead Man's Crossing", in 2002) and the Western Heritage Wrangler Award from the National Cowboy and Western Heritage Museum (for his novel, *Spark on the Prairie: The Trial of the Kiowa Chiefs*, in 2004). A native of South Carolina, Boggs spent almost fifteen years in Texas as a journalist at the Dallas *Times Herald* and *Fort Worth Star-Telegram* before moving to New Mexico in 1998 to concentrate full time on his novels. Author of dozens of published short stories, he has also written for more than fifty newspapers and magazines, and is a frequent contributor to *Boys' Life*, *New Mexico Magazine*, *Persimmon Hill*, and *True West*. His Western novels cover a wide range. *The Lonesome Chisholm Trail* is an authentic cattle-drive story, while *Lonely Trumpet* is an historical novel about the first black graduate of West Point.

The Despoilers and *Ghost Legion* are set in the Carolina backcountry during the Revolutionary War. *The Big Fifty* chronicles the slaughter of buffalo on the southern plains in the 1870s, while *East of the Border* is a comedy about the theatrical offerings of Buffalo Bill Cody, Wild Bill Hickok, and Texas Jack Omohundro, and *Camp Ford* tells about a Civil War baseball game between Union prisoners of war and Confederate guards. "Boggs's narrative voice captures the old-fashioned style of the past," *Publishers Weekly* said, and *Booklist* called him "among the best Western writers at work today." Boggs lives with his wife Lisa and son Jack in Santa Fé. His website is www.johnnydboggs.com.